# CHECKING ON THE MOON

*A Richard Jackson Book*

# Checking on the Moon

## JENNY DAVIS

Orchard Books   New York

The words on page 195 from the song "We Shall Overcome"
by Zilphia Horton, Frank Hamilton, Guy Carawan, and Pete
Seeger, TRO—© copyright 1960 (renewed) and 1963 Lud-
low Music, Inc., New York, NY, are used by permission.
Royalties derived from this composition are being contributed to The Freedom Movement under the Trusteeship of
the writers.

Orchard Books
387 Park Avenue South, New York, NY 10016

Manufactured in the United States of America
Book design by Mina Greenstein
The text of this book is set in 12 point Imprint.
2   4   6   8   10   9   7   5   3   1

Library of Congress Cataloging-in-Publication Data
Davis, Jenny.   Checking on the moon : a novel / by
Jenny Davis.   p.   cm.
"A Richard Jackson book"—Half t.p.
Summary: While spending the summer helping her
grandmother run a small restaurant in a decaying and
dangerous neighborhood on the edge of Pittsburgh,
thirteen-year-old Cab meets many colorful characters and
helps with the neighborhood crime watch.
ISBN 0-531-05960-X.   ISBN 0-531-08560-0 (lib. bdg.)
[1. Restaurants, lunch rooms, etc.—Fiction.
2. Pittsburgh (Pa.)—Fiction.   3. Grandmothers—
Fiction.   4. Neighborhood watch programs—Fiction.]
I. Title.
PZ7.D2923Ch   1991   [Fic]—dc20   91-8284

DON'T LET anyone make you read this. If you want to—great, read on. I hope you like it. But if you don't, don't. It's hard enough trying to write things down without worrying about somebody being *made* to read it who doesn't want to. So good luck. I know for myself what schools can be like, so if they give you any trouble, show them this. I hope it helps.

Washco is a place of my imagination. Any resemblance to people or places, living or gone, is merely that.

Special thanks are due to Judy Johnston and Ann Eames for midwiving. Thanks also to Susie, in whose kitchen it all started, and to my friends, all of them, for support. Thanks to George Ella and Steve Lyon, Anna Stillner, Julie Falk, Boone Davis, and Richard Jackson for reading and feedback. Thanks to Willie for scrambled eggs and energy hugs. All thanks really go to God.

*Jenny Davis*

*Moon, moon, bright and silvery moon,*
*Won't you please shine down on me?*

*from* "Mister Moon"

# *one*

I SAW A MOVIE ONCE that ended with a family in their backyard playing volleyball. The camera captured each person in turn hitting the ball, sending it over the net. And then suddenly the action stopped and the screen showed only the ball suspended in flight. That was the end. The ball never came down; it just hung there.

That's what my life was like last summer. It seemed to me I had been tossed up and, like that ball, whacked hard and sent soaring. Then left to live that way, just up there and hanging.

I'd lived all my life in one place—Blue Cloud, Texas, which is basically a little crook in the road up in hill country above San Antonio. I mean, it's barely a town. I was born there, delivered by Jesus Hernandes, the taxi driver whose vehicle I am named for. Mom considered calling me Jesus, and—no offense intended—thank God she didn't. She could have named me something normal, but no. My mother's the sentimental type and felt she had to mark the occasion with a name. My name. Cab.

My mother goes by her initials, J.L., so maybe odd names run in the family. My father's name is, or was, depending on his status, Duke. How my brother Bill got off so easy I'll never know. I also have—face facts—a stepfather, Jacob Vinter. I suppose that's fairly normal, at least as far as names go. And Jones, my last name, is about as normal as you can get. Or common. I wonder, if a thing is common, does that make it normal? Or, if something is normal, does that mean it's common?

Normal is not my family's strong point. Half my problem is, I can't figure out what normal is anymore. The other half is that I used to know. Or thought I did, which amounted to the same thing, except for one point. I was wrong.

Last summer Bill and I went to live on Washco with our grandmother, while Mom toured the "capitals of Europe" with Jacob. Washco is in Pittsburgh. People refer to it like it's a town of its own, but it's not. It's a neighborhood, and the name of the street that runs through the middle of it. Washco is where my mother grew up, and where my grandmother still lives. I'd never been there before, never met my grandmother, and only found out a week earlier about these summer "plans." (*Plans* sounds like a word that people work out together, which was *not* the case here. This was definitely not a choice situation.)

This tour Jacob had been invited on was some sort of big deal. "Highly select," I recall Mom saying. As if I cared how select or how high. Anyway, they decided to do it, go play the capitals of Europe. But they'd decided at the last minute.

Which meant I found out on the *last day of school* that the summer I had planned was not to be. I'd assumed I'd be at the pool, hanging out with Gretchen and the rest of our group, not doing that much maybe, but doing it together like we always did. So sue me, I was wrong.

I came home that day so happy. No school for three months. No more eighth grade ever! God, I felt good. And there sat my mother at the kitchen table, home early, which if I'd been thinking might have warned me something was up. But I walked into it a complete innocent. Kissed her, even.

Then I saw her fingers. They were plucking at this scarf she had on, and it set me on edge. Pluck. Pluck. "What?" I asked, and she told me.

"You and Bill are going to stay with my mother this summer." Her voice sounded bright and unnaturally cheerful. "Your grandmother needs help, and . . . it's time you-all got to know each other." A lame finish if I ever heard one, but hey, who asked me?

"Your grandmother needs help," was what Mom said, but that wasn't the full story. The truth was, Mom needed someplace to dump me. My grandmother runs a little restaurant on Washco called

EATS. I was supposed to work for her, while Bill, it turned out, was going to get an early start on college by taking summer classes at Pitt.

Jacob isn't my father, as I mentioned; he's my stepfather, and in case you never heard of him, I never had either. But he's famous—at least in certain circles. Jacob Vinter. He plays piano, classical stuff with orchestras.

(My real father, Duke, left Blue Cloud before I was born and hasn't been heard from since. The way I look at it, it's always possible he might have amnesia and one day he'll get over it and show back up. I'm not saying it's likely or anything, but he might.)

I was twelve when my mother and Jacob met and got married—like a zipper closing, *zzzrp*, it was done. I realized then that unexpected things can happen. I just somehow didn't realize the extent.

One night at dinner—a very average night (a rather average dinner too, if I remember)—Mom mentioned she'd been invited to some cocktail party in San Antonio to meet Jacob Vinter before some concert. This meant *nothing* to me. Zip. But Bill must have heard of him, because I remember he joked, "Don't shake his hand too hard, Mom. I'd say his fingers are insured." Turns out they actually are.

So, okay, she went. I spent the night at Gretchen's and had fun. We stayed up talking. Had I known ahead of time it was going to be the last night of my childhood, I would have tried to do something a little more, well . . . memorable. But I had no idea.

When I got home the next day, Bill met me at the door and briefed me as best he could in two seconds. "Fasten your seat belt," he said. "Prepare for lift-off."

I had no idea what he was talking about and only the space between the front door and the kitchen to wonder. Then I saw Mom. She was sitting at the kitchen table, but just barely. Excitement was making her shimmer.

"I have news," she said.

"What?"

"I'm getting married."

I felt the air go out of my lungs and felt something—my heart?—slam once against my chest.

"You are?"

She nodded yes, her eyes bright, face shining. She looked so happy. I felt Bill's arm go around my shoulder, and I leaned in his direction. He scooted his chair closer to mine, and I slumped against his shoulder for support.

*Meeting Jacob has been like nothing so much as being in the path of a meteor—heat and light and utter sparkle. And knowing at last—it is him.*

So reads a fragment of Mom's diary. Yes, I read it and, yes, I'm ashamed of myself, but there it is. And yes, I'd do it again if I thought it would help.

But it didn't. Not really. Nothing did. *This love is something precious*, she'd written. *To be tended and honored. What if we only live once?*

I don't remember much of that first "conversation." Mostly I remember the shock and Bill's shoulder. Mom and Jacob met at this party, fell in love, and decided to get married—all within six *hours*. Now, ask yourself, is this *normal*? Then, to prove they were "mature" or something, they waited six weeks before actually tying the knot.

"Well, we're none of us getting any younger, Cab," I remember Mom saying one of the dozen or more times we discussed "it" before the wedding. "I know I'm setting a bad example for you-all as teenagers, because I think teenagers should take things slowly. But Jacob and I are not teenagers, and I am here in this world—I hope—to do something more than set an example. I would like to live my life to its fullest. Marrying Jacob is part of that. This is important, Cab. This is love."

We met Jacob that same day. He struck me then as he does to this day as a quiet, private man. He is small—Bill was taller (even then) by at least five inches; and Jacob's past fifty, which seems a little old to *me*, but goodness knows nobody asked. He almost always wears a suit and tie, even on the weekends, and when he goes out he wears a hat. He looks like somebody out of a Humphrey Bogart movie. He was born in some country in Europe that doesn't exist anymore—Bavaria, I think—and he has a funny accent.

Jacob's kind of shy really, at least with me. With Bill too, although they always seem to find things to talk about, like farming or World War II. Something. He looks at Mom like he doesn't know where she came from but he's glad she's there. Okay, so I'll admit it—those two are crazy about each other.

Actually, I like Jacob, which is just as well since nobody asked my opinion one way or another. It would probably be easier if he were merely a wicked stepfather; then I could hate him, hate my mother for marrying him, hate all the changes that started when he came into our lives, and get on with things. I could feel one way about it and be done with it. But very little that's happened to me in the last few years lends itself to singular feeling. I don't feel one way about virtually *anything*. Confused? Okay, so I admit it.

I happen to know that, even though Mom acted like she was so sure of what she was doing, she was also scared to death. I heard her talking on the phone one night, late, and thought—correctly—I had heard her crying. I crept out of bed, and yes—face facts—I picked up the phone in her room as quietly as I could and eavesdropped. Reprehensible, I know, but there it is.

She was talking to my aunt, her sister, Sister Ann, who's a nun up in Maine. Mom said, "What if I'm

making a terrible mistake? I'm so frightened, Mol."
(Molly was her name before she became a nun.)
Mom was crying away and talking at the same time.
This was still three weeks before the wedding, and
I got my hopes up that maybe she wouldn't go
through with it.

Then my aunt, instead of pouncing on this perfect
opportunity to make Mom reconsider, said, "Well,
J.L., I did the same thing."

Mom was snuffling. "You did?"

"Sure. I married somebody I have practically
nothing in common with, whom I barely know,
whom Mama disapproved of, and whom I love
madly. I say, God bless you both and good luck."

Mom laughed and said (at least this is what I think
she said), "Luckily Mama doesn't disapprove of Jacob as much as she does Jesus."

Since you know me now for what I was then, an
eavesdropper and a spy, I may as well include some
of Mom's version. From her diary. *Bill has been
sweet. He told me yesterday, "Like the coach says,
Mom, 'Take your best shot.'"* *Unlike Cab who has
been a perfect* crab *about the whole thing. Poor child.
Never did like change.*

Is that such a crime? I mean it. Okay, so she's
right about that, but really, so what? Frankly, I
didn't even think it was *legal* for parents to get married without at least *consulting* their children, but—
face facts—it is.

My mother and Jacob got married, as planned, six weeks, to the day, after they met. The wedding was attended by a whole mess of friends and relations on both sides, most of whom were at least doubtful, if not downright disapproving, of the match. None so much as me, but then, no one else had so much at stake. I kept wanting to know what was going to happen. To me. To us.

Back then, all Mom would say was, "Nobody knows the future, kiddo. Don't be such a worrywart." That was her big complaint about me. I worried too much. I used to think a worrywart was one of the beasts that lived in the scrub, like a warthog only more nervous.

Eventually I just put the whole thing out of my mind. I completely ignored it. It wasn't that hard to do since Jacob saw us only on odd weekends, and everything else stayed the same. He kept his apartment in New York. The times Mom traveled with him for concerts to New York, Chicago, San Francisco, she'd come home raving about the "sights" and I'd get kind of uneasy, but nothing you could put your finger on. When Bill announced he'd won a scholarship in agriculture to Wisconsin, I got scared all over again, but he told us about it in January and he wasn't going until September.

I knew something was going to happen and I knew, by then, having learned the hard way over the marriage business, that I would be informed, not consulted. But as long as Mom kept going to work and Bill and I were in school, I put the uncertainty out of my mind and went on with life as I knew it.

Gretchen, who is going to be a psychologist, said I repressed it. That sounds like ironing something twice, which I can't imagine doing. Anyway, it's true I just kind of forgot about it for weeks at a time.

"It's either repression or denial," I remember Gretchen telling me one of the few times we discussed my inability even to *think* about the future. She enjoyed analyzing my mind, which, according to her, was rich ground. (I believe that is a compliment.)

"What good would it do anyhow?" is what I wanted to know. "I have no control over what happens next. I don't even have a say, as far as I can tell."

"It's a major stressor," she'd agreed sympathetically. And then, because Gretchen was not merely understanding but a good friend, she'd change the subject.

Jacob is, according to the Washington *Post*, a "genius of world-class proportions." When I first read that, I imagined this huge man who had an elbow in Italy and a leg in Argentina. But Jacob is small and bent and all in one place. My point in bringing this up is, I had figured that a genius of world-class proportions would probably not be wanting to settle in Blue Cloud, Texas. And as it turned out, I was right. But they'd been married a year, and nothing big had really changed. Until Washco.

Face facts—there's no way I could have been prepared for Washco.

# *two*

I REMEMBER THE NIGHT we arrived. I woke up somewhere in West Virginia thinking, Oh, shut up! Even before I opened my eyes, I could hear my mother yakking away in the front seat to Bill.

"This is Morgantown coming up. We're getting close," she said. "I'm *so* excited. This time tomorrow I'm going to be over the Atlantic. Can you imagine?"

I could hear Bill in his low, reasonable voice say, "You've said that twenty times today, Mom. Maybe twenty-five."

She laughed. "I can't help it. I'm all keyed up. Things are happening so fast."

"That's true for all of us," he answered, and I swear, although my eyes were still closed so I can't know for sure, I would swear Bill tossed his head just the slightest little bit toward the backseat, meaning me. Meaning don't forget it's happening fast for her too. I can just see him doing it. Even with my eyes closed, I knew Bill.

I knew too the sun was going down. I could feel the chill purple dusk beginning to gather. For three days we'd been driving. Tonight we would arrive.

I was mad. But after a week of fighting, I was also sick of being mad, sick of being anything. I was sick of my mother, sick of myself, sick of being a "typical" teenager. I was caught in a cliché, which made me madder and sicker, but there it was.

Bill is five years older than I am, and he was taking this in his usual even, low-key way. Of course, he was going to be on his own in September anyway. So the bigger issue, which loomed right there whether Mom wanted to admit it or not, the issue of what would happen when summer was over, that question didn't have the same urgency for Bill as it did for me. Plus, once we got to Washco, he was taking classes at Pitt.

I was going to work. "Think you can wait tables?" Mom had asked me.

"Yes," I'd said, but could I? I'd never done it. There was so much I just didn't know.

It must have been almost nine. I'd been sleeping for maybe an hour or more with my cheek pressed up flat and cold against the window, and I woke in stages. Wanting Mom to shut up was first. Then I felt the stiffness in my neck and shoulders. I could hear the swish of trucks passing us. For a long time, I just sat there, awake, but not much. It was pleasant in some kind of depressing way to have my head bounce and bump slightly as the car went over dips.

It didn't hurt really, but it felt pathetic somehow, and that matched me.

I sat propped up there feeling the deep-boned weariness that seemed to have seeped into me as we crossed the country. I was tired, and the more I dozed the worse I got.

When I did open my eyes, I saw this huge blue-gray stretch of mountains and valleys, and I remember thinking that nobody lived in West Virginia. And then there was this house, standing all white and proud and painted, nestled alone in this hillside with cows grazing nearby. Like a picture in a book, the windows were lit soft yellow; clothes still hung on a line near the back door. I took all this in in a moment, and then, as we sped by, I turned and watched it recede into the distance until I couldn't see it anymore. The house was gone, and whoever lived there was gone too.

It seemed to me that night that everything I knew was speeding by, dropping off, disappearing around some corner, into some fog. Things were slipping away—not just places like that house, or our house back in Blue Cloud, but people too, like my friend Gretchen. And that scared me most because if people could slip by, that meant what? Face facts—I could too.

Up front my mother was talking fast and high like she does sometimes when she's wound tight. Her voice, just the sound of it, got on my nerves.

"Honey, quick, look at the map," I heard her say to Bill. "Do we stay on this road or get off?"

I could see the back of Bill's head as he ducked down to consider, could hear the wrinkle of the map. That map had a red line on it drawn from Texas to Pennsylvania.

"Stay on this," Bill said. "It goes all the way to Pittsburgh."

"Are we lost again?" I asked, and my voice came out rusty and thick from not using it.

"No, we're *not* lost again. Are you awake back there? And it's not like we've been lost all that much. Just that once in Arkansas," Mom said quickly.

"Don't forget Houston," I reminded her.

"Oh, well. Anyone could get lost in Houston. All those one-way streets. And it was rush hour. It could have happened to anybody, Cab, absolutely anybody."

"For three hours?"

"Oh, don't exaggerate."

I was not exaggerating, and it irritates me no end when she accuses me of it. She does the opposite of exaggerating. She shrinks things, minimizes them. It was three hours, but, hey, who really cares after a while. Right?

Before we could start arguing, Bill said, "Mom, I hope you know your way from Pittsburgh to Washco because I don't see Washco on the map." He was squinting at it in what little light there was left.

"No problem," she said, and laughed a little. "Why, I could find my way to Washco with my eyes closed. Some things you never forget. Anyway, it's just spitting distance upriver past downtown."

"That's a *disgusting* expression," I told her, and meant it.

"You're right," she agreed happily. "It is." She was in the kind of good mood that no amount of grumpiness on my part could faze.

Although it was true I'd been mostly quiet for those three days in the car, I was not, as Mom insisted, giving her "the silent treatment." I really didn't have anything left to say, and I had a lot to think over. I admit I took a somewhat perverse pleasure from watching her try to draw me out. My mother's a social worker and a pro at drawing people out. But I'm a social worker's daughter, which means I know a few things myself about "interaction."

I knew she wanted me to argue with her some more. She wanted me to voice my objections so she could reason with me, show me *her* point of view. But I'd had an overdose of her point of view in the last week, and wanted no more. The fact was, like it or not, I was going to Washco.

When I asked her flat-out what was going to happen after the summer, she said, "I don't know," and that scared me because I believed her. She really didn't know.

When I was little, she'd tuck me in at night. I

remember seeing her face block out the light as she bent down to kiss me. Her hair would graze my cheek. "Tell," I'd say, and hold on to her sleeve. Back then she knew what to do. She'd sit and hold my hand, rub one side of it with her thumb, and little by little she would go back over the day, setting it straight, smoothing it out.

"First you woke up, remember?" And I would. "You had strawberries on your cereal for breakfast, and got dressed all by yourself." And when she was done with today, she would lay out tomorrow, like clean clothes waiting for me. "We'll get up at seven. You can wear your new shoes." I used to know what was going on, and I liked it like that. So sue me, I miss it.

"This trip to Europe is going to be our real honeymoon," Mom said in a dreamy voice from the front seat.

Barf, I thought, but said nothing.

"Life is change, Cab."

My mother had become expert at pretending I was holding up my end of the conversation even when I wasn't. "The world isn't going to stand still just because you don't like the way it's turning." More philosophy.

Shut up, shut up, shut the hell up! I screamed at her mentally. I saw her trying to catch my eye in the rearview mirror, and for a moment I was afraid I'd spoken aloud. I looked away, found my flashlight, and hunched up with my book.

Bill turned in his seat and asked, "So how's it going back there, Cabbagehead?"

I shrugged, and he nodded like he understood, which I believe he did.

He turned the radio on low, and soft music filled the car. We crossed the Pennsylvania border in a gathering dusk, none of us saying a word.

# three

THE FIRST TIME I saw Washco I thought I was having a bad dream. I mean I really *hoped* I was sleeping. I seriously wondered if Mom was pulling some elaborate joke and this was the punch line. I didn't get it, but, hey, it wouldn't matter—it would be a joke. Except it wasn't.

When you drive into Pittsburgh, at least the way we went, you come through this long tunnel. Now, if you've ever spent most of three days in the backseat of a station wagon traveling cross-country, you know a tunnel is no big deal. But for me it was the last tunnel; we were there, or nearly so. Dread and excitement were both mounting.

When you come out of the tunnel, you're in the middle of all these bridges going over rivers. You're basically *in* downtown Pittsburgh with its lights and skyscrapers. It's a surprise coming out of the tunnel like that and landing smack in the middle of the city.

I'd seen plenty of skyscrapers back in San Antonio, but in Texas they spread them out. These were all squinched together, practically on top of one another on this little triangle of land, downtown. It's called the Golden Triangle.

Pittsburgh is famous for having three rivers, and for being the birthplace of the Ohio. When you come out of the tunnel, you're right above all three of them. It's a good view, but of course we were moving at about fifty miles an hour so I didn't get it for long. We turned upriver and drove a little while through the night.

"These rivers used to be lined with mills," Mom said. "They belched smoke twenty-four hours a day. 'Course it would be dark at noon, but now look. This is all that's left." She sounded sad and a little bewildered.

I did see a mill in the distance, a huge dark sprawling thing that seemed to stretch out a very long way. Its smokestacks blew nothing that I could tell. It looked dead. These rivers were bigger by far than what we had back in Blue Cloud. Barges rode the black water with lights winking.

At other stretches along the bank there were long sandy patches with nothing on them. "That's where Jones and Laughlin used to be," Mom said, pointing to one of these. "My father worked there, and it's gone."

"Life is change, Mom," I reminded her as sarcastically as possible from my post in the backseat.

"So it is," she said lightly. "So it is. And goodness

knows old Washco's seen its share of it." Then suddenly she said, "Okay, everybody, sit up. This is it!"

We'd crossed back over one of the rivers and headed up a steep hill. The street, Washco Avenue, seemed to go literally straight up for blocks. "Saint Catherine's," Mom said, nodding as we passed a large turreted church on our left. "This is Washco, kids. My old stomping grounds." Her voice was rising with excitement, and I sat up to look around. "There's my old high school."

Towering above us on the right was a big yellow brick building. Some of the windows were boarded over, and sprawls of orange and green graffiti, much of it obscene, decorated the sides. Fascinated, I quickly read what I could, but despite the novelty I was filled with a growing horror at the sheer bleakness of the place.

Across the street from the school—all of this on a slant, remember, because we were going practically straight up—were stores. Some were boarded over. Others looked deserted or almost so. I saw a dusty used furniture store, a Woolworth's, a bar (complete with a drunk stagggering around out front), an ancient-looking movie theater with a half-lit flickering marquee: the Centralia.

Garbage scudded across the street borne by a sudden wind. The whole place looked dirty and worn-out. We passed a little fire station, brightly lit and tidy, looking pathetically out of place. I saw two red trucks inside, but next to it stood a vacant lot rimmed in wire and full of odd-shaped, jagged metal scraps. I got chills. Was that a rat running off in the shadows?

There were old, dilapidated houses built tall and thin with brick, wood, and tar paper. They perched on the side of the hill, looking ready to topple any minute. In fact, as I turned in my seat and looked down toward the still-winking lights of the river, I had a wild image of the whole street, our car included, sliding into the black water and being swallowed.

"Mom! This is a slum, for God's sake. A *slum*."

"Oh, well, now. I wouldn't go that far, Cab. It has gone down a ways, quite a ways. That's for sure. But I wouldn't call it a slum. Not exactly." Despite her words I could hear the doubt in her voice. She hadn't seen this place for thirteen years.

We passed a crowd of teenagers standing in the flickering fluorescent light of a gas station. I slumped down, shy of being seen even though it was dark and we were merely a car passing by. Whether they knew it or not, we were neighbors now. I saw a beer can being passed and registered black leather jackets. I felt sick.

"Look up that street." Mom pointed to a narrow road, one of several that led off Washco up to the right. "That's where we used to live—before Dad died. We had a yard and everything. An apple tree. A sandbox even." I could hear memories crowding in; her voice became light and sounded surprisingly young.

I thought fleetingly of our little pink stucco house in Blue Cloud. There, we had nothing but yard, miles and miles of it.

Toward the top of the hill, Washco veered to the left and dipped sharply down. The surface changed from asphalt to cobblestone, and I could feel our tires bumping. Two blocks down, the street bottomed out. There was a flat place with a little concrete playground and a library. I learned later it was the old turnaround for the trolley. Now a narrow road wound past it, up a hill, and curved out of sight.

Halfway down the first cobblestone block, Mom pulled the car over and parked. "Oh, boy," she said ambiguously. "Here we are." She turned off the engine and fluffed her short dark hair with her fingers.

I looked around.

EATS stood crowded between Mondelli's Groceria on the corner and a cluttered shop called Hannah's. There was also Johansson's Shoe Repair and a closed-up dentist's office on that block. In the window of the restaurant, between two pots of straggly geraniums, I saw a hand-lettered sign that read GOOD HOME COOKING.

As I said, I'd never seen my grandmother. But I had seen a picture of her. It used to stand on a bookcase in the living room. Now and then I'd look at her and think, That's my grandmother. I wasn't particularly curious about her. Back then I didn't know her and I didn't think about her. The picture shows a squat old woman with cropped gray hair, a large nose, a sharp mouth, and twinkly eyes. (You can't really tell the twinkle from the picture. I didn't know about that until I met her.) She's wearing a housedress of indeterminate pattern, with an apron over it and a button-down sweater over that. She's standing outside of EATS, and she must be looking into the sun because she's squinting.

That's much as she looked the first glimpse of her I had, except she was inside the empty restaurant, washed in stark fluorescent light, arms crossed and squinting, but this time, squinting into the dark.

"Here we are," Mom said again, unnecessarily. "Come meet my mother, and—well—see where I grew up." I could feel Mom trying to meet my eye, but I avoided contact.

"Better lock it, Cabbagehead," Bill said kindly, as I emerged stiffly from the backseat. His eye I did meet, sought it even as I did so often back then, and it told me, in the swiftness of a glance, that, yes, this was a big deal, I wasn't crazy, or not measurably, and he was there if I needed him.

Bill. All that in a moment. And to think how close I came to losing him.

Mom pushed open the restaurant door, and for the first time I heard the swish of air and chime of the bell that signaled someone coming into EATS. "Hey, Mama," I heard her say softly. I was still on the sidewalk breathing the sharp night air. ("Breathe," Gretchen had said. "When things get bad, breathe.")

"Hey, yourself, June Louise. Hay is for horses, girl, and I know for a fact you weren't raised in a barn. Hah." The old woman's voice was gruff and throaty. She had a way of slipping up on a word that made it almost musical, but roughly so. Everything about her seemed rough at first.

"Oh, Mama, it's good to see you."

"Come here, you rascal," her mother said, and then they were hugging and laughing and crying a little too. My mother is head and shoulders taller than her mother.

"Don't tell me this is you, Bill," the old woman said, disentangling from Mom's arms and looking up at Bill, who is nearly head and shoulders again taller than Mom.

"Hello, Gran," he said warmly, and stooped low to kiss her cheek.

"You were *five* last time I saw you."

"I remember," Bill said, smiling.

"You're full grown." She turned to look at my mother. "J.L., he's a man!"

Mom smiled too. "I know."

I stood in the doorway, neither in nor out, standing like a crane, scratching the back of my left leg with my right foot. Bill pulled me in by the elbow, and I entered stumbling. I shot him a dirty look, but he merely smiled some more, acting innocent.

"So this is Cab," my grandmother said when I had back a bit of my balance. "Hello, Granddaughter," she said formally in her bullhorn of a voice. "And welcome."

"Hi," I said, unable to think of any more to say. I felt shy around this old, squat, squint-eyed stranger who called me Granddaughter and was now studying me intently. I mean, hey, who wouldn't?

"J.L.," she said, and then stopped, as though she were going to ask a question but thought better of it.

"I know, Mama," Mom answered as though she'd heard what was unspoken. "It's true. She's you all over again. I've been seeing it for years."

"Is that what ya think 'tis?" my grandmother answered with a twitch of her lips. "And here I thought she was just uncommonly good-looking."

I realized sickly they were speaking about me. I looked at my aged relative, her face work lined and worn, carved through with wrinkles. Her nose wagged largely between sagging cheeks, and her ears were long and flabby. Her white hair was thick, dry, blunt-cut, and short. I may not be a beauty, but I don't look like that. Just then she caught my eye, and that's the first time I saw the twinkle.

"Anybody hungry?" she asked.

"I'm always hungry," Bill answered honestly.

"I can well imagine that. How'd you go and get so *big*?" she said, looking up at him fondly.

She and Mom got busy behind the counter, and

with a shock I saw that my mother knew exactly what to do. She worked beside her mother easily, getting out plates and glasses, pouring coffee and milk as though she'd worked there every day. I was seeing a part of her I'd not seen before, the part that was daughter.

Bill and I sat at the booth nearest the door. There are only three booths in all, and a table by the window with a red-and-white-checkered cloth. Each was set with a napkin holder, a sugar bowl, and salt and pepper. I counted ten stools at the counter. We ate Irish stew that night and were given, as is everyone who eats at EATS, mounds of white bread and butter. Homemade.

When we finished, I sat there idly, tracing a water mark on the linoleum with my finger, listening as my mother and grandmother's voices filled the air with their reunion music. They spoke rapidly, barely taking turns, sliding up and down melodious scales of talk and laughter.

"You okay?" Bill asked.

I shrugged.

LATER I WAS SHOWN UPSTAIRS and into the front room that was to be mine. It used to be my mother's. "Oh, this is perfect," she said when she looked in on me. Perfect for what she didn't say, and I was too tired to ask. More accurately, I was too tired to listen to whatever her answer might be.

My room over EATS was narrow and very plain.

There are three rooms upstairs and a bathroom. Mine was the smallest, smaller even than the bathroom, which was twice as big as what we'd had at home. Home. The very word hurt to think, and I tried not to.

The bed, a youth bed really, took up all of one wall. My mother may have fit it perfectly, but when I tried it out I found my feet crowding the baseboard. Had she heard these same squeaks and groans when she shifted about?

Across from the bed stood an old battered dresser with a faded mirror above it. I studied my face carefully, and found, to my relief, no signs of resemblance to my grandmother. My nose is a bit big, but is not, I firmly trust, as large as hers. By a long shot.

Looking at myself in that blurry mirror, I realized that twenty years ago it had been my mother's face reflected there, her face at twenty-one. I tried to imagine what she looked like, but I couldn't. She'd known my father then. They'd met in college, at Pitt, where Bill was now going to start classes.

My parents had married and moved to Blue Cloud, which they'd picked off a map "on a whim," sitting in the student union building. They liked the name, my mother told me once, and my father said he wanted the light they have in Texas. For painting. Twenty years ago.

Had he left Blue Cloud on the same kind of whim that took them there? I don't know. He took off the same day my mother found out she was pregnant with me. She was at the doctor's getting the news: he was home packing. I could feel rejected about that, but I don't. Technically, he didn't know about me. Of course, he did know about Mom and Bill, so it's a little hard to figure.

He wrote her a note that I've seen. "J.L., honey, I'm gone." That's all. It's been folded and refolded dozens of times over the years. The paper is dry now except for a grease spot where some butter got on it once. It's one of the few proofs I have of my father's existence. His leaving.

I have one other—a painting he did of Bill. In it, Bill is four years old and standing in the field outside our house—no, face facts: what used to be our house—in Blue Cloud. He is dancing with a wildcat cub. The two of them are shoulder to shoulder. The field is burnt yellow like Bill's hair, and the sky is twenty shades of blue the way it is in Texas. The wildcat is the color of the scrub behind them, and at first you might miss it and think it's just a painting of a towheaded boy in a yellow field. But then you see these two cubs, locked in an embrace, and for me—well, I get a thrill of fear, wildness, and delight.

That painting tells me my father was a good artist. I hope he still is. And of course I know Bill survived the embrace. If you didn't, you might be left with the fear, because there in the farthest corner is the slightest suggestion of what might be the mother cat.

Mom said it really happened. They were sitting in the kitchen and looked out the window. There was Bill dancing with a wildcat.

I don't know why my dad left, and if Mom knows she's never said. When I was old enough to notice about fathers—that most kids had them—she gave me the painting. I was five then, and I've grown up with it ever since. Later, when I asked more questions, she showed me the note and said she didn't know where he was. He'd been gone seven years and by law he was considered dead. But, as I say, he might not be. I kind of like to keep the possibility open that he might show up. He might. You never know. The best thing about not having a father is the possibilities. But maybe I have too many possibilities to be normal. Maybe that's the problem. Maybe being normal is being certain, and I can't say I'm that. But maybe that's what it really is, a kind of confidence.

I suddenly wondered whether this same mirror had been on the wall thirty years ago, my mother's first night here. Had she wondered what was going on? What would happen next? I knew she had. She'd been eleven when her father died and she'd moved in over EATS. Her father was injured in an accident at the mill (the mill, or what was left of it, that I'd seen at the bottom of the hill). For the first time, what had been just a family story took on location and reality. He'd lingered, from what I'd heard, for a few months before he died. Long enough to sell their house and buy the restaurant. Then, after he died, my grandmother moved in above it with her two girls: my aunt Molly, the present Sister Ann, and J.L., my mother. Thirty years ago.

While I stood peering into that old mirror, I realized that my mother's life too had thrown her unexpected punches. Some of them below the belt. One surprise after another. Is that what life is?

I'd been deluded into thinking life was predictable by having twelve steady years that flowed mostly just one day into another like a smooth stream. Just Mom and Bill and me. Then all hell broke loose. First she got married, now this. Off to Europe, and then what?

"Things happen. Sometimes they seem fair—sometimes they don't." How many times had I heard her say that? Now this was happening to me. I wanted the grace to handle it with dignity, but grace was beyond me.

There lodged in my chest a lump, not a figure of speech, but a real, hard thing that wouldn't break up, that put a constant pressure on my breastbone. I didn't want this, any of it, but it was mine nonetheless.

I turned away from that mirror with older eyes. The furniture in the room seemed full of history and significance, but in a code I didn't know yet how to read. That night I unpacked and put my things into the drawers that had been empty twenty years. There was no closet, only a rod stuck in a corner near the door. On the floor lay an oval-shaped braided rug whose original colors were impossible to guess.

I hung my father's painting on a nail above the bed and wondered if he'd be able to find us if he came back to Blue Cloud looking.

Mom's old desk stood facing the window. I rummaged through it, of course, searching for clues, but came up with only paper clips, a leaking cartridge pen, and seventeen cents in change. The wood was nicked and stained from age and use. In one corner, in tiny letters, she'd written the word HELP. Just that. HELP.

I wondered about that. About her.

In the room next to mine I heard my mother and grandmother talking. Softly now, but still talking. Bill would take Mom to the airport the next morning. She and Jacob were "rendezvousing" in New York. We wouldn't see her again until late August. And then, "We'll see," she'd said, as though that were really some kind of plan.

So I was in a state of shock, as who wouldn't be? "Sulky" was how Mom put it, which I personally didn't appreciate at all. "Moody" was Bill's word for it. "Watch out for those moody blues, Cabbagehead," he'd said to me that night in Arkansas when he'd caught me crying outside the motel-room door.

We were at a Red Roof Inn. He'd come out to get a soft drink. I was on my way back from getting one when I was hit by a wave of loneliness and fear so intense it wrung sobs out of me before I knew it. It just hit me—or I hit it. Like walking into a wall. I don't cry much and I don't cry easy, but I was crying that night alone in the dark.

He put his arm around my shoulder and walked me down the stairwell till we stood near the gate of the little kidney-shaped swimming pool. The water was pale blue in the moonlight and perfectly still.

It was exactly a week to the day after I'd come home from school and learned we were leaving. I was intensely homesick for Gretchen, worried about Washco, and basically terrified of the uncharted lands that lay beyond. The future.

I don't know how much of this Bill knew. Mostly I think he is wise in a rare and beautiful way. That night he showed me the moon. It was there, almost full and very clear just then, passing between some wispy clouds. We could see it reflected in the water of the pool, which lay still at our feet.

"See that?" he asked, pointing up to it. For a long time we just stood there and looked at it, neither of us saying a word. "We all look up and see the same moon," he said at last. It was comfort as best he knew how to offer, and I accepted it as best I was able.

It was certainly some kind of comfort that Bill was going to be there with me in Washco. He had accepted this move for the summer with his usual calm equanimity. I trusted that if he was letting this all happen, it must be basically okay. I took my lead from him as much as possible, but I was also well aware that he was off to Wisconsin come September.

Now, in Washco, I looked again for the moon, but could not find it. I left the window open to catch what breeze might be blowing up from the river. The room was stuffy and hot. All night long I heard cars passing, doors slamming, snatches of radio music and laughter. It must have been very late when I finally drifted off. What sleep I managed was sweaty and worried and restless.

# four

EATS OPENED at six-thirty every
morning except Sunday, when it was technically
closed. My grandmother was usually up by five,
lighting the oven, setting out dough to rise, putting
on coffee, looking at the paper. "Puttering," she
called it.

I woke dull and irritable at seven and lay listening
for sounds of life. I could hear the bell below clang-
ing and knew customers were already coming and
going. The sound of television morning news came
from somewhere. The knot in my chest had pulled
very tight overnight and it ached. Remembering that
I was there "to be a help," I got up and dressed.

Outside my room was a little central hallway with
two staircases, front and back. The front led straight
to a private street door, while the back, which was
narrow and twisty, went to the restaurant's kitchen.
It was down this that I ventured that first morning.

The kitchen at EATS is large and full of corners

and always warm. Sunlight poured in through a window high in one wall, illuminating the huge black ovens. Off to one side stood a wooden table with two stools and a rocking chair pulled up next to it. Along one wall were shelves stacked with restaurant-sized cans, boxes, and big glass and plastic jars. There was also the largest refrigerator I'd ever seen, silver and built into the wall.

"Ahh, there you are," my grandmother said, coming through the swinging doors that separated the kitchen from the restaurant. "Good morning to you, girl."

"Good morning," I answered.

"How'd you sleep?"

"Fine," I lied.

She smiled at me a little, or at least her mouth twitched in what I took for a smile. "I'd say it's a bit noisier here than what you're used to. And no cows, of course."

"Cows?"

"Well, don't you have cows in Texas?" she asked in that gruff way of hers.

"Yes, well, of course we do, but they don't roam the highways at night." I'd said it haughtily, but was then, as though in punishment, assailed by a memory of lying in bed at home in Blue Cloud hearing the cattle low, deep in the night. I winced with homesickness.

"No," she continued as though she were really thinking about it. "But then I'd say the cows don't stay out drinking in the bars till two o'clock either. Am I right?"

I had to smile. "Uhh . . ." I hesitated because I realized I didn't know what to call her. "What should I do? To help, I mean."

"How about if you start by seeing who needs their coffee warmed up?"

I was relieved to have a job I was fairly certain I could manage. "Uhm, do I look all right?"

Her mouth twitched again, and she surveyed my blue jeans, sneakers, and T-shirt. "You look fine to me. Why? Were you figuring on a uniform?"

She'd guessed my thoughts with worrisome accuracy.

"Tell you what." She turned away and reached for a starched white cook's apron hanging from a hook by the stove. "Put this on, and it'll look more official-like."

The apron came to my ankles. "I don't think so," I told her, feeling ridiculous.

"Right. I see what you mean. Here's how you do it." Even though her hands were knotted by arthritis, she tucked the material up and tied it slowly but deftly at my waist. Now the apron came only to my knees. "That's the ticket," she said, standing back a bit and looking rather pleased with her work.

"One other thing," she said as I turned to go. "Mac out there, he's the policeman. He don't get more than a half a cup refill. Got it?"

I nodded yes.

"Doctor *told* him to lay off the caffeine six months ago, and he ain't done a very good job of it." She gave me a wink and bent down to look into the oven, checking on her pies.

There were three customers. The two women sitting in the middle booth didn't speak to me as I refilled their cups. Mac sat at the counter, looking much too large for the stool he perched on. I eyed his cup surreptitiously and decided to wait until he asked to offer him more.

"So you're the little one come in from the wild west," he said to me in a low but nonetheless booming voice.

"Texas," I answered.

"Oh, yes. Texas. You've had some great criminals in Texas."

I was uncertain how to reply to this and settled finally on "Thank you."

"So now you've come east to see what's left of the big city. Is that it?"

"Sir?"

"The late great remains of the city on the three rivers."

I felt confused. "Is it over now? The city, I mean. Seems like we saw plenty of it driving through last night."

"Oh, well . . ." He shook his head at me. "I suppose it's got some life in it yet, when you see it like that, but not around here. The city your grandparents and I knew, mind yer, that's been gone a long while and no coming back." He smelled his coffee and sipped it. "A lot of things changed when the mills went out."

"Did you know my grandfather then?" I asked without meaning to or even knowing I was going to.

"Lord, yes. I knew Oscar back when I was still in short pants. He was older than me. Heh! Funny you should ask." Mac looked not at me, or his coffee, but into the mirror that lined the wall behind the grill. "I looked up to him, see. Didn't follow him into the mills, though, notice. No. Went into the force instead." He gave his uniformed chest a substantial thump. "From this distance, it's hard to say which was more dangerous."

I nodded and thought about this. I liked the way he talked to me, although it made me nervous, him being a policeman.

"So hit me," he said suddenly.

"Sir?"

"My coffee." He gestured toward his empty cup.

I took the pot down and carefully filled it halfway.

"You got a problem with your eyes?" he asked. His badge flashed in the early light. "That's only half full."

I felt incredibly nervous. I had had little experience disobeying adults. Especially adults in police uniforms. In fact I was trying to obey my grandmother but couldn't think how to explain all this. "I don't think so, sir," I said as politely as I could.

To my relief he chuckled. "She already put you

wise to me, did she? Oh, well." He looked rather mournfully at his half-full cup and took a deep swig.

"So you know my mother?" I asked, again not really meaning to.

"June Louise? Heh. I saw her christened, saw her graduate high school, and I was at her wedding. The first one, that is. Yeah, I know your mother. So you're J.L.'s girl, the one with the funny name. What is it?"

"Cab. Cab Jones."

"Right. Where is she, anyway? I was hoping to catch a glimpse of her."

"She's still upstairs," I said. Then, "She's going away, you know. To Europe."

Did he hear the bitterness in my voice? The accusation? I know I did, and felt ashamed of it, but there it was.

He answered mildly, with a laugh somewhere underneath the words. "So I hear. Went and married a genius, didn't she?"

"Yes, sir, she did."

"Well, you tell her old Mac sends his love."

He put several dollar bills by his plate, picked up his hat, which had been parked on the stool next to him, and stood up. He was bigger than I'd even suspected and moved with a slow lumbering walk. I watched him out the door and saw him cross the street, heading toward the library. He stopped to tip his hat to someone I couldn't see and continued on his way.

*40*

My grandmother came through the swinging doors and showed me how to use the cash register. I liked its bright ring, liked plonking the green receipts on the spindle next to it. I liked too the weight of coins in my hand, and the crinkle of bills. Feeling a bit like a person in a play, a person playing "cashier," I took the two ladies' money and made change carefully.

"Why, you're catching on already," my grandmother said in an encouraging way when the ladies left. "I can't tell you how much I appreciate you coming like this, Cab. Thank you."

Did she think I'd had a choice? My face reddened with embarrassment. Luckily some more customers came in just then, and that awkward moment passed.

She showed me how to set up the silverware and water for each person. I cleared dishes, wiped down the counter, poured coffee, and generally had no trouble staying busy until Mom and Bill came down.

Mom looked beautiful, I have to admit. When shampoo bottles use the word *radiant*, that's what they're talking about—the way she looked that morning. Glowing. She was dressed in a suit, a new blue suit that I'd never seen, and she wore gold earrings that made her look rich.

I felt stricken. It suddenly hit me—no, of course it wasn't sudden; I'd known it all along—but it hit me hard then that she was really going to leave. Leave *me*. She looked indecently happy, considering the circumstances. My grandmother told me to go sit down and eat.

"I can't think of what all to tell you two," Mom said as she sat across from Bill and me in the booth. She sipped her coffee, regarding us steadily, eyes shining. "Seems like there ought to be some parting words of wisdom, something." She smiled, and I felt sick.

"Well, let's see." Bill considered. "You ought to tell me not to forget to check the oil in the car."

"Good point," she agreed. "Don't forget to check the oil."

"And you better tell the Cabbage here to brush her teeth *right*, no fooling around." Bill smiled at me, and I squirmed unhappily.

"Teeth. Absolutely. What else?" Mom asked.

"Help your grandmother, both of you. Don't stay out till all hours of the night. Change your underwear. Come on, Cab, what else?" Bill nudged me with his elbow.

"Don't spend all your money in one place." I recited it like a litany, playing along in spite of myself. "Wash behind your ears whether you think they're dirty or *not*, tie your shoes, brush your hair . . ."

Mom began to laugh. Bill picked it up. "Look both ways before you cross the street, any street, don't play the radio too loud, cover your mouth when you sneeze . . ."

"Don't forget to say please and thank you. Eat

your vegetables, spinach too. Use a fork and a napkin at every meal."

"Clean out the tub. Don't leave hair in the sink."

"Make sure your socks match, and don't chew your nails, at least not in public."

"Don't drink, don't smoke, and don't gamble," Bill chanted.

"Don't run around with wild women unless you absolutely can't help yourself," I said, and started laughing.

"Don't take candy from strangers or wooden nickels from anyone."

"Don't swear, don't lie, and don't whine."

"Be good, be kind, be careful."

"And in other words," Bill and I finished together, "be perfect!"

Mom was laughing so hard tears began to stream down her cheeks. "Okay, you turkeys, I give," she choked, putting up her hands in surrender. Bill caught my eye and grinned. For a moment the three of us sat in perfect harmony, the smells of sugar doughnuts and coffee mingling with our smiles.

And then it was time for her to go. The laugh we'd shared made it a little easier to say good-bye. At the last minute I even managed to mumble, "Have a good time."

"I love you," she whispered, and was gone.

# *five*

IF WORK IS SOME SORT of balm for
the troubled soul, I should have been in great shape.
There was more work running a coffee shop than
I'd suspected, and my grandmother kept me busy,
beginning that very first day. I did dishes, swept
floors, waited tables, wiped down counters, carried
out garbage, cut potatoes, apples, carrots—there was
always something to cut, sometimes my fingers—
ran errands, and generally made myself useful. The
first week was the hardest, physically. I was beat
like a drum by the end of every day, and sank into
grateful oblivion every night, despite my creaking
bed and sticky sheets, despite the shrieking streets.

I worked mornings, from seven till noon, then
had the afternoons to myself until about four, when
I came back to help with dinner. We closed at eight,
sometimes earlier. Bill was gone most days to the
university.

EATS was a kind of central station for people on

Washco. We didn't do a big business, but it was steady; and because most of the customers were friends or near neighbors, I soon knew many of them. Being "Mrs. Doyle's granddaughter" lent me immediate acceptability, especially with the old people. Of whom there were many on Washco.

Mac came in every morning for his coffee and doughnut. He told me stories of famous criminals from the "olden days." He especially liked Billy the Kid. Mrs. Mondelli, who loved to talk, and her husband, a singularly silent man, ran the groceria next door. I was in and out of there several times a day, and she was in and out of EATS just as much. I came to enjoy the familiarity. The Mondellis looked a bit like a pair of old crows; both had raven-black hair now dramatically streaked with gray.

Hannah owned the junk store on the other side of EATS and came in every day, if not to eat at least to say hello, drink coffee, and collect and pass on news. Besides selling junk, she told fortunes. For a dollar she would tell people where to look for lost keys or rings. I've seen her do it. She was a big brassy woman, and because she had a gold tooth that flashed like a lighthouse in her mouth, I assumed she was a gypsy. She owned a real crystal ball that she showed me one day, although according to her she could also read tea leaves, cards, and especially palms.

Hannah offered to tell my fortune for free the first time we met, but I pulled away in something like terror. I was afraid to know. I didn't believe she really could see the future, but just in case—or anyway, or something—I wouldn't let her do it. I shied away from her for a while and made sure I kept my hands palms down when she was around.

Mr. Johansson ran the shoe-repair shop two doors up. I met him my third day on Washco, when he glued a loose flap on my tennis shoe for thirty-five cents. He was tall and thin and white-haired. He too was very old.

The bus stopped right outside of EATS, and there were a number of people, mostly older women, who were in the habit of coming in for pie and coffee after work. They came to sit and collect themselves, to rest their ever-weary legs before they started the walk home. I soon knew all of them by sight, if not by name, and knew a bit about their jobs and their families. I learned a lot from them too about corns and varicose veins.

Shakespeare came in every afternoon about three-thirty, only he was on his way to, not from, work. His real name was Cranston Oliver, but my grandmother never called him anything but Shakespeare, because—as she ruthlessly reminded him and he shyly admitted—he was a writer. He was also a teacher, employed by the city, and ran the Community Education Project in the basement of the library.

From the first time I met him, I could tell my grandmother had a soft spot for him. She had his coffee poured and the cream set out even before he walked in the door. She watched for him to get off the three-thirty bus. My first day at work, he came in wearing a raincoat and didn't bother to take it off. He sat at what I learned was his customary seat, the fourth stool down from the cash register.

Unlike most of our customers, he wasn't that old, no more than thirty anyway, although he had a patch on the back of his head that was balding. I watched him blow on his coffee and saw his glasses steam up. He took them off and rubbed the bridge of his nose.

"Burning the midnight oil again, and don't tell me no. I can tell by the bags under your eyes," my grandmother said, making it sound like an accusation.

"I'm afraid you're right, Mrs. Doyle. Again." He had a slight southern drawl, and his words came out slower than most people's up there.

"You're keeping irregular hours," she said as though this were a crime. Then, "Eggs?"

He smiled. "Please."

She turned to the grill to start cooking them; he pulled a newspaper from his coat and began to read. Neither of them spoke as the eggs sizzled. I was sitting, for what I believe was the first time that day, at the table by the window, sorting silverware.

"Shakespeare"—my grandmother waved her spatula at him and ordered—"turn around and say hello to my granddaughter, Cab Jones. Cab, this here is Shakespeare."

He swiveled on his stool and nodded to me. "Pleased to meet you. I'm Cranston Oliver."

My grandmother gave a throaty chuckle. "Huh. Now ain't that fancy, and to think I known you all this time and never knew it."

"Well, Mrs. Doyle," he said, turning back to her with a slight bow, "it gives me some relief to think there are still one or two things about me you *don't* know."

Just below the surface of their banter ran a strong stream of affection. I could feel its presence easily despite the words.

"Huh," she said again, and put before him a thick white plate with his eggs and toast. "I'll tell you one thing I *don't* know is how you think you're going to hold on to your health keeping the kind of hours you do. You ever hear of early to bed, early to rise? Or don't that apply to you educated people?"

"I'm sure there's wisdom in that, Mrs. Doyle, but a man's got to have some time to work on the Great American Novel." He used a mocking tone that made me think he was serious. "Mine just happens to fall in the middle of the night."

"Huh," she answered shortly.

He turned his attention to his eggs and toast. When he finished, he pushed his plate aside and she refilled his cup. "So whaddya know?" she asked flatly. It was the question she put to all her regulars, and they to her. Even that first day I'd heard it a dozen times.

"Well, let me think." He put his glasses back on. Glancing at the paper beside him, he said, "Taxes are going up again."

My grandmother snorted in disgust. "So tell me something I don't know. Since when did they go down?" She sat on her stool, which she had pulled up behind the cash register. When she sat in the shop, and mostly she didn't, that was her place.

Shakespeare said, "Seems to me, Mrs. Doyle, to return to an earlier subject, it's tolerably hard to tell you anything you *don't* know. You keep a pretty sharp eye out from your perch right here."

My grandmother looked modestly pleased. "I try," she said simply.

"I will tell you this, though it's doubtless old news to you. We're offering a class in t'ai chi this summer." He pronounced it "tie chee." "It's an ancient Oriental form of exercise and self-defense. For *all* ages," he added, looking at her speculatively.

I realized he was hoping she might be interested. Huh, I thought to myself.

"You going to teach it?" she asked.

"Oh, no, I wouldn't know how. There's a Mr. Alec Su who's offered his services. *If* we get enough enrollment." He paused.

She pushed herself up to her feet and took his plate.

"Where's he from?" she asked.

"Squirrel Hill, I believe. He teaches chemistry at Pitt."

"No, I mean like China or Japan?" she said irritably.

"I don't really know, come to think of it. But he's highly recommended, and he seemed like a nice man. I met him last week. We need ten people, minimum. For the class." You could hear the question in his voice, but she ignored it.

"Huh," she said.

He had turned around some on his stool and was gazing out the window, past me. "You know, in China," he said in a lazy, conversational tone, "in China, people of *all* ages get out in the parks and do these exercises together."

"Fancy that." I saw her mouth twitch.

"Yes, people of all ages," he repeated.

"Well, now. I think I saw something about it on TV one time. Yes, out in a park, or a square I think they call them. Everybody waving their arms around real slow. Looked like they were ready for lift-off. You gonna take it?"

"No, I'm teaching pottery at that time. It'll be Wednesdays from seven to eight. *If* we get the enrollment."

He reached for his wallet, and my grandmother wrote out his ticket in seconds, her pen whizzing over the little green order pad she always carried in her apron pocket.

"I wish I *could* take it," he added, handing her money and laying down a tip. "It's supposed to be an excellent form of lifetime exercise." He stressed the word lifetime.

"Get outta here," she said affectionately.

He smiled and rose to leave. "Tomorrow," he said, addressing me, "I'll bring you a brochure and see if there's anything *you'd* like to take. One Doyle a day is all I can tackle."

I was so startled I dropped a fork. "I'm a Jones," I mumbled, picking it up. "Cab Jones." For some reason I felt hurt that he'd forgotten my name.

"I'm so sorry," he said. "Of course. Good day, Mrs. Doyle. Cab. Jones," he added with a small smile.

"Bye."

"See ya, Shakespeare," she said roughly.

He left, as everyone did, to the swish of the door and the clang of the bell. He did bring me a brochure the next day, and I looked it over as respectfully as I could before handing it back to him. "I'm not much interested in continuing my education right now," I told him. "It's summer." He didn't argue.


I MET LUCY that first week too. Lucy ran a Salvation Army center for the homeless. It was in an old storefront on a side street, one block over from the library. My grandmother was in the habit of sending a box of pies and any other food she had extra once or twice a week. One day she sent me to deliver it.

The building was easy enough to find, as it had a big red sign on the front. Inside was one large room with stained yellow linoleum on the floor. Along one wall stood a couple of long tables and folding chairs; on the other, a television set with a sagging couch and some plastic chairs in front of it. A few people were watching a game show and looked up at me when I entered, but they showed no interest and immediately looked back at the show. A baby crawled around on the floor wearing a diaper, nothing else.

Lucy came from behind a desk in a corner I hadn't seen at first. "You must be Cab," she said, smiling at me and taking the box I was carrying. She introduced herself and thanked me profusely. She was in her twenties, I'd guess, with soft brown hair pulled back in a loose bun. "Please thank Mrs. Doyle for me. For all of us. That blueberry pie she sent last week was a treat bar none. You can't imagine how grateful we are."

"You're welcome," I answered uncomfortably. My eyes kept darting around the room, trying to take in everything. I saw a man sleeping in a corner, sitting up. He was unshaven and looked sick and dirty. He snored some, and a little drool ran down one side of his mouth. I stared so hard I knew I was being rude, but I couldn't help it. Lucy let me look, and said nothing. I left quickly.

Later I asked my grandmother, "Where do the homeless people come from?"

"From all over. From nowhere. They're just people down on their luck. Times are hard."

"Do they live there? I didn't see any beds."

"The beds are in the back. But nobody lives there long. Mostly they're just people passing through on their way to nowhere else. Every now and again, Lucy finds someone a job or gets them into one of these so-called training programs."

"She runs it? The center, I mean."

My grandmother nodded. "She's got some kind of mission, poor thing. A little like my Molly. Your aunt. It's her calling is what she told me once. I guess it is. She's a nice girl, though. A bit touched"—she pronounced it "teched" and tapped the side of her head—"but, hah, I ain't one to hold that against a person." She gave me a quick wink.

There were other homeless people on Washco, people who slept on the street. During my free time (when I was free to do *what* was the question), I walked a few times down to the river and back. One day I saw a man curled up near an air vent, covered in newspapers. It was near the Woolworth's. I thought he was dead. I went over to him, not sure what to do, but sure I had to do something. When I drew close and bent over him, I could see he was breathing and could smell the stench of him, cheap wine and urine mixed. Some people walking by flicked their eyes in his direction and kept walking. After standing there a moment, I did the same.

There was an old lady with a shopping cart who

regularly rummaged through our garbage. It gave me a terrible feeling to see her do that.

At the end of my first week I wrote a long letter to Gretchen trying to describe this "other world" I'd fallen into. I'd gotten one short, unsatisfactory letter from her that left me feeling hollow and alone. She was spending her days at the pool in Blue Cloud, exactly as I had expected to.

# six

THERE DIDN'T SEEM to be anybody my age on Washco. In Blue Cloud, even though we lived out in the country, I'd had pretty many friends. Here I had no one. I sometimes saw groups of teenagers, as I'd seen that first night. But there was no way I could imagine breaking in to such a pack. I didn't even want to. They scared me. Mostly they stood on the corner up the street from EATS, smoking, passing time, yelling things at cars or at one another. Walking by, I felt young, and I hated that feeling.

One day, after I'd delivered some food to the center, Lucy asked me if I'd like to take the baby to the playground. "Her mother's sick, she's sleeping, and I can't really leave right now, but I was thinking maybe . . ."

"Sure, I'll do that," I told her, really rather glad to have a way to fill an empty hour or two. "What's its name?"

"Her. It's a girl. Named Marvel," Lucy said.

"Marvel? Like the comics?"

"Yeah, but it's no joke." She gave me a tired smile and called to the baby, "Marvel, come here, sweetie."

The baby looked around. "Can she walk?" I asked.

"A little, but she still prefers to crawl. I've got a stroller you can use. She loves the swings." Then, "You know about babies?"

"Some," I told her.

"Marvel is almost two. She probably should be walking by now, but she's a little slow that way." Lucy picked the baby up. Her face was smudged with dirt, as were her legs. "It's hard to keep a baby clean in a place like this," she said to me as though apologizing. "Here, you hold her and I'll get her things."

I sat down and held her on my lap. Marvel was chubby but very still. "Hey, baby," I said. She turned to me with the most serious brown eyes I'd ever seen. She didn't smile or make any sound. I bounced her on my knee, and she swayed a little. Lucy came back with a washcloth and a little sunsuit. Even while her face was being scrubbed, Marvel didn't change expression.

Marvel did like the swings, or at least I think she did. They had the kind for babies with a bar, and I hefted her into one of those and gave her a push. Something that might have been a smile spread across her features. She looked like a little Buddha, very fat and solemn. As we were alone on the playground, I tried singing to her, little baby songs, nonsense. She didn't cry, so maybe she liked it. I don't know. With Marvel it was hard to tell.

I tried to get her on the slide, but she was too heavy for me to lift up the ladder and she had no interest in climbing it herself. After a while, I put her back in the stroller and took her to EATS.

My grandmother's eyes lit up when she saw us. "Well, who have we here?"

"This is Marvel," I told her, feeling somehow rather proud of her, as though she were mine. "Her mom's sick. They're staying at the center with Lucy. I took her to the playground."

"Sit, sit. It's hot out there. How about some lemonade?"

"Yes. Wonderful. What about ice cream? Do you think she's too young for ice cream?" I asked.

"I've yet to meet the child that was too young for ice cream, Cab, but maybe she ain't supposed to have it."

"Oh, yeah, maybe not."

"But applesauce now . . ." my grandmother said.

"Sure, what could be wrong with applesauce?"

"Right, and how about some ice cream for you, Granddaughter?"

"Thanks—" I almost said, "Thanks, Grandmother," but I stopped myself. Even after a week I hadn't settled on what to call her.

We didn't have a high chair at EATS. Used to,

but it wore out, according to my grandmother. "Don't get many babies in here nowadays," she said. So I sat with Marvel in my lap—a still, solid weight who ate applesauce like she knew what she was doing. She followed the spoon intently and never spilled a bite.

"Here you go," I crooned at her, hoping for a smile. Just one.

"And here *you* go, honey," my grandmother said, imitating my accent as she delivered a dish of vanilla ice cream with chocolate sauce on top.

I smiled.

"Let me finish up with Miss Marvel here, and you eat your own," she said, and sat down beside me in the booth. She took the baby with evident pleasure and fed her what remained of the applesauce, neatly wiping Marvel's mouth with a napkin when she was finished. "It's been a while since I held one this size. She's a quiet thing, ain't she?"

I nodded. It felt comfortable sitting there beside her.

"Uhm," I started.

"Uhm?" she asked, and I could see the twinkle in her eye.

"Did you have any brothers and sisters?" I asked. Mostly I was making conversation; it wasn't something I'd wondered about much.

She sighed. "Oh, yes. I was one of eight."

"Eight?" That seemed a large number for a family.

"Indeed. But three of them died before their second birthdays. And the rest—well, they're all gone now."

"Oh." I'd heard the sadness in her voice. For a while we just sat there.

"Cab?" she said at last. I looked at her. "Would you like to call me something besides Uhm?"

I blushed and turned my face away. "Like what?" I mumbled.

"Oh, I don't know. I *am* your grandmother, you know. You could call me that. You and Bill are the only two in this world who own the right." She paused, and I didn't say anything. "Course, you could call me Maddie; that's my name too. Or, well—what would you like?"

I considered. Bill called her Gran, and it rolled off his tongue easy as anything. I had tried, but hadn't been able to get it out. Nothing came easy to me just then.

"Grandmother." I said the word slowly, testing out its awkward edges. They seemed to fit. It was a hard word to own, but as she said, I had the right. "Maybe I'll call you Grandmother."

She nodded. "I'd like that. If you can."

Grandmother, I thought again to myself. Grandmother mine.

SHAKESPEARE CAME IN for his three-thirty breakfast and duly admired the baby. "And is she?" he asked when I'd told him her name. "A marvel?"

I considered. "We only just met this afternoon. Mostly I'd say she's still water."

He cocked his head at me and looked puzzled for a moment. "Oh." He smiled. "Still waters run deep, is that it?"

I nodded.

Grandmother handed her back to me and began to push herself to her feet. Shakespeare took her arm and helped her. I tucked Marvel into the stroller and cleared the dishes from our booth. "I'd better get a move on. Lucy might be wondering."

"Have you been by the library yet?" Shakespeare asked. He was holding the door for me as I maneuvered the stroller.

"No, not yet," I admitted, hoping he wouldn't pursue it.

"Well, stop by sometime. I'll try not to be educational."

I laughed and said good-bye.

On the way back to the center I saw Mrs. Mondelli. She admired both Marvel and me. "Nice to see a young face around here once in a while," she said as she finished pinching my cheek. Up until then I'd only read in books about people who pinch cheeks. Mrs. M. was the first person I met who actually did it, and I'd find myself bracing to get it over with whenever I ran into her.

I asked Lucy whether there was something wrong with Marvel. She looked at me through narrowed eyes and said, "Why do you ask?"

I hesitated. "She just seems real quiet."

Lucy eyed me steadily, then blew a long stream of air through her teeth. "You may know more about babies than you think. Of course, she could just be a quiet type, but to tell you the truth, yeah, I think there *is* something the matter. Marvel is what the doctors call 'developmentally delayed.' In regular words it means she's slow, maybe real slow."

"Oh." I felt a sadness weigh on my shoulders as if a heavy quilt had been draped there. I was sorry I'd brought it up. We watched Marvel crawl over to the TV area. "What do you think?" I asked at last.

"Me? Well, I'm not sure I know all that much about it, but it seems to me she might just be, well, depressed. She and her mother have had a very hard time. Very." She blew more air through her teeth. "I'm afraid to think what that might mean."

Afraid or not, it seemed to me Lucy thought long and hard about the people who came under her care, especially the children.

In a way she reminded me of my mother. Mostly Mom didn't talk about her work, but sometimes it came home anyway. I remember vividly the day I found out what child abuse was. I was eight, and it was long before she became the wife of a genius of world-class proportions. She'd come home in a rage the like of which neither Bill nor I had ever seen before. She drove up scattering gravel and screeching rubber. Mom? She stomped off to her room and started throwing what we found out later were shoes at the bedroom door. Then something crashed, and Bill couldn't take it anymore. "Mom, are you all right? Mom?"

At first we heard this muttering, then the door opened, and she stuck her head out and looked us over as if she knew who we were but not very well. "I'm feeling a little emotional" is what she eventually said, and in the silence that followed, her words struck all three of us as faintly hilarious.

We went into the living room and sat down. Mom leaned her head back, sighed raggedly, and rubbed at her eyes.

"I worked a child-abuse case today that was uglier than my worst nightmare," she said finally.

"Oh," Bill said, and nodded. He understood, and his face looked suddenly tired.

To him she said, "I have to wonder, on a day like today, if I'm cut out for this job." She'd been a social worker since she'd first come to Blue Cloud. Personally I couldn't really imagine her being anything else. "I know you're supposed to have compassion for these people. I know most child abusers were abused themselves and blah, blah, blah. But if you could *see* what this *monster* did to this baby. Oh, God."

"What are you talking about?" I asked. "What happened?"

She looked at me a longish moment and swallowed. When she continued, it was in that calm teaching voice she used for explaining things.

"Some people, Cab, some people have very big problems. Very big. It's like they're not all there. No." She shook her head vehemently, her short curls flying. "This guy's all there, but he's . . . he's rotten. I hate to tell you this, but it's a fact of life, I'm afraid. Some people are rotten, sick. Really twisted. This guy, oh, he's vile." The last word came out like a shudder.

"Who is?" I persisted.

"This man who abused his little girl. He's her father, but he did terrible things to her."

"Like what?"

I saw her glance at Bill, who met her eyes. His face was still, and I could read nothing there.

"He burned her," she said in a shaky voice. "On purpose."

Bill flinched. I waited. Then finally, through clenched teeth, as though looking at a picture in her mind, Mom said slowly, "He put her on an electric burner. You know, on the stove. He held her down and burned her bottom. Her little thighs and in between her legs and her fanny. Third-degree burns. That poor little thing. She's only five, but five's already so old. When I think of the pain, the terror she must have felt. And to think that she'll remember. Oh, God."

I felt awful. I could feel my own bottom burning and could imagine the little girl's agony all too well. I knew now why Mom was so upset. Bill looked like he might throw up.

I moved over to where she was in the big armchair and climbed on her lap. "Why did he do that, Mom? What did she do?"

"That's just it. Not a thing in this world. She didn't do anything wrong. It wasn't her fault. Not at all."

"But why? Why did he do that?" I remember feeling, at eight, that if I could know the why of a thing I'd be all right.

"Because he's a sicko is why, Cab. He's rotten, like I said. Because . . . I don't know why. But he did it. And I didn't stop it in time, damn it. I'm not Superman. Things get by me. We had a referral on them over two years ago. If . . ." She suddenly beat with her fist on the arm of the chair. "If, if, if. To hell with it. It didn't happen that way. They're flying her to Houston right now. They have a good burn unit there. Maybe she'll be okay."

I sat in her lap and listened, understanding little, but taking in her exhaustion, her rage and despair. That's how I learned what child abuse was. It gave me a new persepctive on fathers. I'd never imagined, living with my mother, that parents were capable of such horrors. It simply hadn't occured to me. Much less as a Fact of Life. There were worse things than having a father who ran off before you were born. There was child abuse.

Being a social worker was hard on my mother, but it was work she loved. From time to time throughout the years of my childhood, she would come home and stomp around in her room, throw shoes at the door, although I never saw her in quite the same rage as she was that day. I could tell that Lucy's job was hard on her too. I couldn't quite imagine her throwing shoes at her bedroom door, but you never know what people do in the privacy of their bedroom.

# seven

THEN ONE NIGHT—I'd been at Grandmother's a little more than a week—I was in the
kitchen washing pots and pans. Most dishes we did
in the metal sink under the counter out front, but
pots and pans were cleaned in the big double sink
in back. I was scrubbing away, wishing for a window, anything besides that plain brick wall to look
at, when Mac came rushing past me, making me
jump. I dropped the pot I was washing and splashed
water on myself. He wasn't wearing his uniform,
which startled me all the more.

"Stay here, and lock the door behind me," he
ordered as he ran. The whole room seemed to shake
with his weight. He threw open the back door,
yelled, "Go on, lock it," slammed it shut behind
him, and was gone—down the steps and into the
alleyway.

For a dumb moment I just stood there, my hands
still in the dishwater. Then I quickly ran to the door

and threw the bolt. For good measure I pulled the chain across as well. The kitchen door has a small window in it, and I peered through it into the gathering dark. This was early June still, and the days were long, but our little passage of narrow sidewalk that ran between Washco and the back alley lay mostly in shadows. I could see nothing.

I shivered then, thinking without wanting to that maybe someone out there could see me. The kitchen seemed suddenly cold and frightening. I wiped my hands and went through the double doors to the shop. Grandmother stood alone at the cash register, but I could tell from the swish of the door that someone had just left.

"You lock it?" she asked, holding out an arm to me. I nodded yes and went to her. She folded me in and gave me a hug. We were just the same size.

"What's going on?" I asked, not at all certain I wanted to know.

"Street crime, darling," she said. "There was a mugging up the street." She eyed my wet apron as though it told its own story.

"A mugging?" I repeated. "A holdup?"

"Yes, something like that. Mr. Johansson got hurt. You know him. Two doors up."

I nodded yes and unconsciously wiggled my toes in the sneaker he had fixed.

"Let's hope he'll be okay. Hit on the head, though, which is never good." She sounded very old and tired. I glanced at her face, which looked a mass of wrinkles just then around her thinly creased mouth.

I thought of tall, straight, white-haired Mr. Johansson, thought of him hit on the head, and winced. It must have been a tall mugger.

Grandmother was closing the cash register. "Don't you go fretting, Cab," she said. "I know you ain't used to this, but it goes on all the time."

"It does?" I asked in surprise. I certainly was *not* used to it.

"I'm sorry to say that it does," she said sadly. "Not that it always used to be like this, mind you. Not a bit of it." She let out a sharp sigh. "Why, when Oscar and I were first married . . . huh." She seemed to recall herself.

"What?" I wanted to hear.

"Oh, nothing. I was just remembering something. Plague of the old." She tossed me a grin.

"What?" I repeated. It seemed to me that if she were plagued by rememberings she kept them mostly to herself.

"Well, when we were first married"— she looked a little embarrassed—"I'd walk Washco every night and meet him coming home. Kinda romantic-like, see. Hunh."

I didn't say anything.

"It ain't what would pass for romance in this day and age, but it did for us. All kinds of weather, made no matter. Wintertime too."

Her face looked softer now, less pinched, but then she shook herself and said roughly, "Not anymore, boy, I can tell you. Them streets ain't fit to walk by day, much less at night."

Someone banged on the door. EATS was closed, and we both jumped, still nervous. It was Mr. and Mrs. Mondelli. I let them in, and she was talking as she came through the door. "I made him come," she said as she sat heavily on a stool. "A few steps away and I made him come. Can you believe it?" She slipped her black shawl from her head to her shoulders. "Can you blame me?"

"No, no," Grandmother answered. "Who can blame you? I'd do the same. And, hey, it's not every day I get to see you, Frederico. How long since you had a taste of my pie? Eh? Too long, that's what. Cab, get down that chocolate cream. Can't get this in Italy, you know."

He laughed a soft dry sound.

"Any news?" Grandmother asked.

"I don't know," Mrs. Mondelli answered. "I saw a patrol car headed up street with its light on, so maybe they got him. I don't know."

Mr. Mondelli sat silently beside his wife. He took a bite of his pie and said, "Very good, very good," in his heavy accent. He then ducked his head and busied himself eating. I don't know if he kept more of an accent than his wife because he rarely spoke or if he rarely spoke because his accent was so heavy.

Whatever the case, Mrs. Mondelli did the talking in that family, as far as I could tell.

"What the world is coming to," she said. "*Tcch*. Here I sit afraid to go next door. Mercy."

"It's bad," Grandmother agreed. "I was saying the same to Cab just a minute ago."

Mrs. Mondelli shook her head in exasperation. "I tell you what. Drug pushers, criminals, alcoholics. Lazy bums. That's what it is. These good-for-nothings too lazy to go get an honest job. Sleep late and go hit an old man on the head and take his money. They ought to be ashamed." Her voice had risen as she spoke.

"It's the truth," Grandmother answered. "I'm sorry to say it, but it is."

"Just how much *does* this go on?" I couldn't help but ask.

The two women glanced briefly at each other, then looked at me. "Too much," they said together.

"I know," I said. "But how much?"

They considered the question. Mr. Mondelli finished his pie, laid down his fork, and looked out the front window. It was completely dark now.

"What would you say, Maddie?" Mrs. Mondelli asked after a moment. "Two times a week? Around here, mind you. Just up on Washco. That isn't to say what goes on down by the river, or"—she paused dramatically—"God forbid, in Pittsburgh."

"I guess that's about right. On the average and

getting worse, it seems to me," my grandmother answered.

"Getting worse is right. Mugging, robbery, vandalism like you wouldn't believe. And worse things too," Mrs. Mondelli added darkly. "It's not safe."

Before they left, Mr. Mondelli thoughtfully fingered a leaf of one of the geraniums on the windowsill. "Keep it wetter," he said to me. These were the most words I'd heard him put together at once, and I think the only time he'd ever addressed me directly. I nodded yes to him.

That night, lying in bed, staring blindly at the cracks in the ceiling, I remembered a few words that had passed between Mom and Bill when she'd first told us we'd be coming to Washco. Less than words even, it seemed to me now—looks. Understandings that at the time had passed me by, but that now, terribly, began to make sense. "Your grandmother needs you," she'd said to both of us, but to Bill there had been more. "I'll be glad for her to have a big guy like you coming in and out."

I lay awake waiting for Bill. I finally heard his key in the street door, his footsteps on the stairs. Grandmother must have been waiting for him too. She got up to meet him, and I could hear their voices in the hall, but then she took him into her room and shut the door. Through the wall I could make out only mumbling; then the door must have opened, because Bill's voice became clear for a moment. "I'll be home early tomorrow, Gran. Matter of fact, I'm bringing somebody with me." Grandmother's voice rose with interest, and then they were both laughing. I could hear that, and the sound of it stabbed me. I felt lonely and left out, but also, finally, very sleepy.

The last thing I heard that night was the scream of sirens, off somewhere in the distance.

# eight

THE NEXT MORNING, after the breakfast crowd cleared out some, I was sent to buy flowers. In my pocket I fingered a slip of paper with the name of the hospital where Mr. Johansson was being held for observation. They were holding him because, to quote Hannah, "He *is* seventy-two years old, for God's sake." I couldn't tell from the way she said it whether his age was good or bad, but it was definitely something.

All morning long the regulars (as Grandmother and I thought of them) had streamed in and out, picking up and dropping off pieces of news. Mac *had* grabbed the mugger, and I was right: he was tall. And young, only sixteen.

"He won't do time at all," Mac said disgustedly. Mac had been out walking his dog and seen the attack. "It's a lucky thing I did see it. The guy hit him with a brick," he told us. "A brick. In the back of his head. Seventeen stitches they took, I heard."

"Good night!" Grandmother exclaimed. "He's lucky he's not dead this morning."

"God have mercy," Lucy muttered under her breath. I was just setting down her tea and heard her. Lucy wasn't a regular; in fact, that was the first time I'd seen her at EATS. She'd come, as it seemed so many did that morning, simply to check in, to shake their heads and make the *tchtk*ing sounds of dismay so common on Washco.

"I hate to mention it, Gran," Bill had teased in the kitchen before he left for school, "but from the sound of it in there"—he nodded toward the shop— "crime is good for business."

"Don't even think such a thing!" Grandmother snapped back, and Bill had looked abashed.

Nonetheless, I had been busy and was glad of the break to buy flowers. Washco looked much the same to me that morning as I climbed the hill and started the long descent toward the river. Dirty, worn-out, run-down, and old. From the top of the hill you can see a swath of the river between the housetops.

Suddenly, clearly, something clicked. My vision changed. I saw the layout of the neighborhood for a flashing moment from a mugger's point of view. Each of the many small alleyways running between the buildings was a perfect getaway route—narrow, dark, and lined with trash cans, just right for obscuring a pursuer's path. The streets that intersected Washco Avenue were twisty, steep, and mostly unlit.

For a few moments it was as though I had become a mugger and was planning out my next crime. It was horrible and thrilling.

The idea of bashing someone over the head and taking his money had been utterly foreign to me until then. I had watched as much TV, seen as many movies as the next person, but until the night before I'd never known anyone who'd actually been mugged, much less ever contemplated doing it. Now I could see that Washco, with its large number of tottering old people, was perfect territory for someone young and fleet and ruthless. It gave me the creeps, and I shook myself to clear my head.

No, if I were to be a robber, I'd rob from the rich, not the poor. So I fervently hope. My criminal inclinations, I suspected, lay less toward stealing than snooping. I remembered my mother's diary. And then, with all the force I'd been using to push them away, I was flooded with thoughts of her. For a moment I could almost see my mother's face, especially her mouth, the way she smiled. And then, just as plainly, I knew I'd forgotten her, wouldn't know her if I saw her. It was a tumbled feeling, frightening to think I'd forgotten my own mother's face.

I thought about her being a social worker, knew she worked with "juvenile delinquents" back in Blue Cloud, as well as child abusers and illegal immigrants. I wondered, hard, what she would make of all this on Washco. And then, far worse than wondering, I knew I didn't care. I just wanted her near. Now. And she was so faraway.

She'd written one gushy postcard from London and, just the day before, another from Bonn. The sights! The food! The people! She was all exclamation points and rapture. She knew nothing of Mr. Johansson, of what was happening on Washco, of me.

It's very hard to want someone with whom you're very angry. And I was very angry with my mother, but I nonetheless wanted her very much.

This torrent of thought and feeling left me tired and rather off balance. When I reached the florist's, I had trouble deciding what to get. "Something nice" is what Grandmother said when she pressed into my hands the bills and change that had been collected that morning. I carried twenty-one dollars and seventy-five cents, two dollars of it my own.

Inside the florist's shop the air smelled wet and green. I browsed, enjoying the confusion of color. Behind a glass were tall red and white roses, pink carnations, tulips in orange and yellow and even black. Of course, there were many other flowers whose names I don't know. I was beginning to feel overwhelmed when something caught my eye. There, in a basket near the window, nestled in among bigger, brighter blooms, were bluebonnets. They seemed to be peeking out, as though they were shy.

Texas bluebonnets. A wave of homesickness

crashed over me then. I was very faraway from that hot, dry, yellow and green country I'd grown up in. I bought that arrangement, which, with delivery, came to almost nineteen dollars.

"What kind of card would you like?" the lady behind the counter asked.

"I'm not sure. What do you have?"

"New baby, wedding, graduation, funeral, get well . . ."

"That's it. Get well." I pulled out the paper with the hospital name on it and the room number and gave it to her.

"Here you go," she said, putting a small card and envelope in front of me and handing me a pen.

I hesitated. I wasn't sure I could remember all the names of the people who contributed, and I knew for certain I didn't want to try spelling them. I wrote "Your Friends" under the flowery script that read "Get Well Soon."

"Fine," the lady said, and tucked the card into the basket of flowers. The bluebonnets winked at me, and when the lady wasn't looking I winked back. "These should get there this afternoon. I have a truck going out in a few minutes, and I'll put this on it."

As I started back up the hill, a light rain misted in, blowing up from the river. I felt the wind pick up at my back, felt a sharp quick chill in the breeze and then a steady fine drizzle of rain. It felt good.

On impulse, I decided to go to the library instead of back to EATS. I was free until four o'clock and had no desire to return either to the restaurant, the kitchen, or my small, empty room upstairs.

The library, which has columns and wide front steps, is the most substantial-looking building on Washco, not counting Saint Catherine's. It was built by Andrew Carnegie at the turn of the century, and above the doorway are the words FREE TO THE PEOPLE. It was built to last and looks it, but that day, in the rain, it too seemed forlorn. The wind pushed the swings in the deserted playground next door, their chains clanking out a ghostly melody. It seemed so desolate that I was pleased.

Inside, the floor was marble and the rooms high-ceilinged and hushed. A librarian stood behind her desk sorting books. There was a boy at a table in the corner looking through magazines and a few other people browsing the shelves.

I went first to an atlas that was open on a stand of its own. I turned to Europe and stared at the colored blocks, the funny names and shapes that made up the paper landscape my mother now inhabited. I picked out Bonn in Germany, but could make nothing of it from the map. Standing there, wet and slightly chilled, I realized I needed a way to lock back those feelings of missing her. Mooning over a map was not going to help.

I turned to find the shelves marked FICTION, thinking perhaps I could lose myself in someone else's story. But instead, what I saw was a large black-and-white photograph of *my* block of Washco.

In eerily sharp detail I saw EATS, with Mondelli's on one side, Hannah's on the other, Mr. J.'s right beyond that. The street was deserted except for a parked car. It looked as though someone had stood on the library steps and pointed the camera up the street. I walked closer and read what was written below it. "Washco: a place that used to be—by Tracy Sibowski."

"Well, whaddya think?" a voice behind me asked.

I jumped back and eyed the owner. She was a girl about my height with a mop of light brown hair that hung almost to her shoulders. She had dark, almost black, bushy eyebrows that were raised expectantly. "So whaddya think?" she asked again. Then, before I could answer, she said, sticking out her hand, "It's only fair to warn you, I'm the artist, so go easy."

I laughed, couldn't help it, and shook her hand. There was something so good-natured about her, so playful and direct that I felt immediately drawn to her. "You know"—I nodded toward the picture— "I was just thinking the same thing myself. About Washco. You took it?"

"Sure did." She raised her eyebrows again. "You from the South? You sound like it."

"Well, kind of. Texas."

Her eyebrows, which she apparently used for punctuation, flew up in question.

"I'm here for the summer," I explained. "At EATS."

"Mrs. Doyle's?" she asked.

"My grandmother."

We both looked at the picture again. It was so clear and lifelike I had the vague notion Grandmother might open the door and step out on the sidewalk as she did every day, "taking the air."

"How'd you make it so big?"

"Tricks of the trade," she said modestly. "See, I took a photography class here this spring. From Mr. Oliver. Learned all about it. You know him?"

"I don't think so," I said, then realized who she was talking about. "Oh, Shakespeare. Yeah, I do. That's what my grandmother calls him. He's a writer, right?"

"That's the one. Shakespeare, huh? Hah!" and she laughed in evident pleasure at this newfound nickname. "His place is in the basement. Want to see it?"

We had been standing in the back hallway and carrying on this conversation in the low tones you use in a library. Tracy led me to a wide stairway, and we went down. The basement was huge. She gave me a tour—a coatroom, a classroom, two bathrooms, a tiny darkroom, and a large art room that was set up with a potter's wheel and vats of clay off to one side. Last, she showed me a tiny office, stuffed, from what I could tell by peeking through the window, with papers. Shakespeare's office.

"Is he really writing the Great American Novel?" I asked, with what I hoped was enough teasing in my voice that Tracy wouldn't think I really wanted to know.

"Absolutely," she replied without a hint of sarcasm. "One day I expect he'll be very famous. He's really just about Washco's last hope of getting on the map. And wouldn't you know it, he doesn't even live here."

I'd figured as much, since I'd seen him get off the three-thirty bus every day.

"Of course," she continued, "if he doesn't make it, there's always me. I'm a writer too." Her eyebrows expressed humble acceptance of what was apparently, from her tone, a dubious fate. "What about you? Do you write?"

"Me? Well, sure, I guess so." I thought about the long letter I'd written to Gretchen. "I mean, I could. If I wanted to."

"You ought to sign up for his summer class. Reading and Writing. We've only met one time. I'm sure it's not too late," she said. "Pottery too, if you're into it. I'm taking that with my mother." Her eyebrows wrinkled, indicating something, although I wasn't sure what, about her mother. "She says pounding that clay helps get out her aggressions. And I'm all for that." She smiled. "So whaddya think?"

"I don't know," I said slowly, and then suddenly I did. Tracy was a friend. Here on Washco. "Maybe I will. Hey, why not?" We both smiled.

"So what's your name?" she asked, and I smiled again, because we already felt like friends though she didn't know what to call me.

"Cab."

"Cab? Like corn on the cab? Hah! Just kidding. No offense, I hope."

"No offense taken." In truth it was one of the few puns on my name I hadn't heard before. "Cab like— yellow cab. You know, like a taxi. I was born in one." I felt a little shy revealing this family history, but it was true and I wanted her to know.

"You don't say." Tracy knit her eyebrows. "Cab what?"

"Jones. Plain and simple."

"Well . . ." She seemed to be considering, looking me over. If it was some kind of test, I guess I passed, because she said, "Gosh, I'm glad you're here," and her tone was so warm just then that I was glad too. "This can get to be one boring place in the summer," she added.

I'd noticed that myself. "Must be, if you get so desperate you go to school to have something to do," I said.

"Oh, this isn't anything like school," she answered quickly. "You'll see. Let's go ask your grandmother and then maybe you can come over my house. We only live a few blocks from here."

# nine

THAT'S THE WAY WE MET. By the time we came up the basement steps, we were giggling noisily and won a stern look from a man at the card catalog. We opened the door and took off into the drizzle.

Shakespeare himself was perched on his usual stool, reading the paper and eating his afternoon breakfast. I hadn't realized it was so late. Tracy ran over to him and plunked down on the stool next to his. "I want Cab to take your class. I told her it wasn't too late. It's not, is it? Say it's okay. Please?"

"Which one?" he asked.

"Writing," she said.

"And reading," he amended. I remembered the title from his little brochure—"Reading and Writing: a Class for Everyone."

"Right, of course. And reading," she said, swiveling on her stool to shoot me a grin. "Well, whaddya say?"

"It's not too late," he answered simply, and went back to his paper.

Grandmother regarded Tracy for a long straight moment with an expression I couldn't read. "Would you like a soda?" she asked.

"Oh, yes, Mrs. Doyle, but . . ."

"On the house." She made a little wave of her arm, and I saw her eyes twinkling. "Cab, will you go check those potatoes? Make sure they're not sticking."

The kitchen, as it did so often, had filled with the warm yeasty smell of boiling potatoes. I stirred the large pot carefully with the long-handled spoon, and in a moment my face was wet with steam.

Grandmother came through the double doors and joined me, peering critically into the pot. "So what about you?" she asked, smoothing down my damp hair. "You want to take this class?"

Instead of answering her, I asked, "Do you like Tracy?"

"Who, Pippi Longstocking?"

"Who?"

"That's what I used to call her when she was little. Had braids sticking straight out and, well, all those freckles." Tracy did have a lot of freckles. "Yeah. I've always liked her. Like her mother too. What about you?"

"Haven't met her yet," I said, not sure which question I was evading this time. "I got nice flowers," I told her. "They had bluebonnets in them—

lots of other stuff too, of course. I think Mr. J. will like them."

"I'm sure he will. Word is, he'll be home tomorrow. If you don't mind, I'll be asking you to carry him his meals for a few days. Maybe longer."

"I don't mind," I said, and realized this was true. "I like helping out." This came out in a very small voice, as it made me feel shy to admit it.

Her mouth twitched, and I felt her squeeze my shoulder. "I know you do. So what about this class? You want to take it?"

"I do, but I don't know how much it costs."

"Oh, well, if that's your worry, forget it. Besides, your mother left me plenty of money for things. You've got a well-to-do stepfather now, Cab. Might as well get used to it," she said very gently. I think she realized this was a sensitive subject, despite the fact that we'd never discussed it. "Now I gotta get back out there. What's your answer?"

"It's okay with you?"

She nodded yes.

"It's seven till nine, I think, two nights a week. You sure you can spare me?"

"I'll manage, but we've got to see to it someone brings you home."

"Grandmother! Come on! It's a block and a half."

"Still."

After a brief discussion it was agreed that either Tracy's mom or Shakespeare could see to it I got home safe. I thought of the mile and a half of country road Bill and I walked all our lives in Blue Cloud, from where the bus left us off to the house, every day after school. Here, I could look out the window of EATS and *see* the library, but my grandmother insisted on an escort.

Although Washco and Blue Cloud shared the same continent, the same government, and nominally the same language, I had again that feeling I'd tried to describe to Gretchen of having landed on a different planet.

"We start at seven o'clock," Shakespeare said to me as he paid for his meal.

"Sharp," Tracy added. "No *ish*."

I nodded.

"Do you have a library card?" he asked.

"Uh, no. Not yet."

"Well, you're going to need one. See you girls tonight. And don't worry, Mrs. Doyle. I'll see she gets home safe."

"You do that," Grandmother answered, and punched the cash register, making it *cling* just as he opened the door to leave. That bell joined the door's, and the air was momentarily loud with ringing.

It was time for me to get back to work, but Grandmother said, "No rush," which at least appeared to be true, as the place was empty just then. I took Tracy upstairs to my room.

"You are *so* lucky," Tracy said, as we climbed the narrow, twisting back steps.

"Oh, yeah? How come?"

"I live in a normal house. You know, porch, living room, dining room, kitchen. I've always wondered what it was like over these stores."

I considered my luck. "Well, this is it," I said, opening the door to my room.

"Small, huh?" she said, flopping on the bed.

"Yeah, it used to be my mother's." I sat on the desk, my back to the street.

Tracy looked around. There wasn't much to see. I had added nothing of my own for decoration except the painting of my father's. The room retained its cell-like quality. Tracy pointed to me or maybe the desk where I was sitting.

"You'll need a notebook, you know. For the class. And pencils and stuff. Personally, I type. Been at it since I was seven." She blew a thin lock of hair away from her mouth and lay back on the bed, gazing at the ceiling. "You know, Cab, I just feel like I've got it." Her voice had grown dreamy and thick.

"Got what?" I asked.

"Greatness," she said, and sat back up, propping her back against the wall. "It's a feeling, see. Well, actually it's more than a feeling—it's a conviction. I just know it. I know it all the way through me. Always have."

I couldn't think of any way to reply to this.

"I don't mean it to sound like bragging. I'm afraid it does. Does it?"

"Not necessarily," I said honestly. Honestly it sounded like nothing I'd ever heard before. "Greatness, huh? Like what?"

"Well, that's the part I'm not too sure about. What, when, and how. But the way I see it, those are just details. The main thing is the knowing it. The only thing that worries me is that it might come at the very end of my life and I won't be around to savor it. You know, like what if I pull a little kid out of the path of a speeding car and then get hit myself? That would be great, but then it'd be over. What a drag." Her eyebrows knit in contemplation of this unfortunate possibility.

"I doubt it, though," she continued. "Personally, the way I see it now, I'll probably end up on the stage. Movies would be nice. Though of course I may make it big with writing. I don't know for sure—I just know it's in me."

I sat across from her and stared. Her self-confessed headlong plunge toward glory was something I'd never encountered before. The same impulse that had quickened in me upon meeting her in the library quickened again. This was a friend, and a friend worth having! Her conviction that her life was important electrified the very air around her. In the hour since we had met, I could already feel the difference. I felt myself pulled into a world, or a vision of the world, more alive, more exciting than any I'd been able to conjure on my own.

Maybe it was Destiny. I myself had not considered

Glory or Greatness or Destiny. Jacob's Fame, which was my first real brush with things usually referred to in capital letters, had left me bruised and raw and confused.

"Maybe my life is speeding up," I said, thinking out loud.

"What do you mean?" Tracy asked.

And so I explained, as best I could, how I'd lived all my life one way, in one place, and that now it was over, gone, done with, and everything was new. "It could just be the illusion of speed," I told her after thinking a bit. "Maybe I just notice it all more now because I'm not used to it, so it seems like more."

Tracy listened well. "Yeah, maybe," she considered. "It could also be from working in a restaurant. You see a lot of people that way."

I felt so grateful to her for entering into it with me, for trying to understand. "It's more than that, though," I told her. "Things have changed, big-time." And I explained to her then about Mom and Jacob.

"You mean he's famous?" she asked, sitting up, eyebrows high.

"World-class."

"Wow."

"I know."

"And they got married just like that?"

"Six weeks, to the day, after they met."

"To the day?"

"I kid you not." It felt wonderful to unload this.

"Wow."

"I know."

"Maybe it's not your imagination, Cab. Maybe things really are going faster."

I nodded. "And now Washco," I said, and gestured toward the street. "You know Mr. Johansson?"

"Yeah. I heard about last night. Bad news. My dad's a fireman, and they put the call through for the medics. He told us about it this morning. I want you to meet my family."

We looked at each other and smiled. So she had greatness, I had a mess. We both had something else now—each other.

"Hey, there's Bill," I said as I spied our family station wagon round the corner and start down the hill. "He's got somebody with him. A girl, I think." I was straining to keep him in sight, but he'd pulled into the alley to park as he always did. "Come on. You've got to meet Bill."

We clattered down the back stairs and into the kitchen just as Bill opened the back door. With him was a girl, a beautiful girl. She had long, thick auburn hair and a smiling face.

"Hi, Jessica," Tracy said.

"Oh, hi, Trace," she answered. "How are you?"

"I guess these two already know each other," Bill said to me.

"Well, we know each other too. So I guess it's

even," I responded, grinning. I felt so good, so happy.

Bill grabbed me in one of his usual brotherly head-locks and gave me a relatively (for him) gentle knuck-le rub on the top of my head. "This is my sister, Cabbagehead Jones. Cab, meet Jessica." It's difficult to have much dignity when being introduced to somebody with your head in a headlock. I did what I could.

"Hi," I said, when I'd finally extricated myself.

"I'm glad to meet you, Cab," she said in what was the lowest—face facts—sexiest voice I had ever heard. "Bill's told me a lot about you."

"I hope you know better than to believe him," I said. "He lies like a rug."

She tossed her head back and laughed, a warm and deep, happy laugh. Catching Bill's eye, she said, "I'll keep that in mind."

"So I'm Bill," he said, extending a hand to Tracy, who shook it.

"I'm sorry," I said. "This is Tracy."

"You two know each other?" Bill asked Jessica.

"Sure. I used to baby-sit for Tracy and all the rest of them. How's your family?"

"Everybody's fine. How about you?"

"We're hanging in there."

The kitchen clock read exactly five. "It's time for me to get back to work," I said, feeling important. I pulled the apron from the hook and put it on, folding it over and tying it with the ease of ten days' habit.

"I gotta go too," Tracy said. "See you tonight, Cab."

"Yeah, see you tonight."

# ten

AS BEST I REMEMBER, Grandmother and I served fried chicken and mashed potatoes to the dinner crowd that night. Bill and Jessica sat in the first booth and talked in low voices and small smiles. Grandmother knew her, of course, as she had at least a nodding acquaintance with everyone on Washco.

Jessica worked at the Centralia, the movie theater down the hill, across from the high school. She, like Bill, was taking summer courses at Pitt to help her get a start on college. She intended to be a veterinarian *if*, I heard her say, she could get through calculus.

Jessica was beautiful. I don't know how else to describe her. Graceful. She had a way of making even the smallest motion, cocking her head, unfolding a napkin, look . . . well, interesting isn't quite the right word, but it's close. Alluring, maybe, but not staged. She seemed perfectly natural. Her voice—I said it was sexy, but that's only part of it. I felt like I could sink into it, it was so deep, and I wanted to, it was that inviting.

I found myself trying to lower mine. "May I take your order?" I practiced on each customer in ever-deepening tones. At one point, though, Grandmother put her hand on my forehead to feel for a fever.

"Thought you might be taking a cold from getting caught in the rain," she said. "Sounds like you got a frog in your throat."

There was a tiny television on the wall near the end of the counter. It droned away softly, as much a part of the noise as the clinking of silverware, the talk and the laughter, the ringing of the cash register, the clang of coins and glasses. When the local news went off, I heard Grandmother say to one of the regulars at the counter, "They never said a word about it." I knew instinctively that she was talking about Mr. Johansson's mugging. "Makes you wonder what else goes on they ain't telling us." Both women shook their heads.

By quarter till seven the rush was over, and she sent me upstairs to get ready for class. Okay, I admit it, I was scared. I looked at my face in the mirror, pulled a brush through my hair, and looked some more. My stomach rumbled with nerves; my own dinner had gone untouched. I took a pencil from the desk drawer and a piece of notebook paper. The paper I could fold up and stick in my pocket, but what about the pencil? What was I supposed to do—walk down Washco holding a pencil? And I knew if I put it in my pocket there was a good chance I'd forget about it when I sat down. Then what? Would I have to be taken to the hospital to have lead or graphite or whatever it is they put in pencils taken out of my behind? I shoved it behind my ear.

Grandmother had joined Bill and Jessica in the booth by the time I got back downstairs. She gave me the once-over and handed me a ten-dollar bill. "I can't vouch for anything else about him, but price-wise Shakespeare is really very reasonable." She chuckled at her own joke. "If you decide to take pottery or that, what was it—t'ai chi?—you just let me know."

"Let's see how this goes tonight," I mumbled.

"Hey, Cabbage," Bill said. "Gran said you were taking this class for fun. You look like the under-taker."

"This *is* for fun," I growled at him, and with what I hoped passed as dignity, I told them all good-night.

THE LIBRARY CLOSED AT SIX, so the Community Education students used a side door that led into the basement classrooms. Tracy was waiting for me outside and waved as she saw me coming. I could have hugged her for waiting. She ushered me down the steps and into the classroom we'd seen that afternoon.

Five people sat at school desks arranged in a circle.

Naturally, they all looked at us as we entered. To make it worse, Shakespeare said, "Oh, good. Our new student is here. I believe that's all of us, so let's get started."

He introduced me, and I smiled weakly at the others, not really seeing them. My heart was thumping hard. Tracy pushed me into a chair, which I took with relief. Before she herself sat down, she pounded me proudly on the back and announced, "I'd like everyone to know that Cab is *my* find."

I had a brief vision of myself as a nugget gleaned from a river.

"We're glad to have you, Cab," Shakespeare said, "whoever found you." There was laughter, and I smiled. "Part of what we're doing here," he continued in his slow voice, "is finding ourselves. There's nothing quite like reading and writing to help you discover yourself and the world we live in. And as the course title says, this is a class for everyone. We're all at different levels of proficiency here, and at different stages of life. So be welcome, and be yourself."

This whole little speech had been said in my honor, or at least in my direction, so I nodded and tried to look like I had some idea of what the hell he was talking about.

"Now," he went on, addressing the rest of them, "would anyone like to share their writing assignment from last Thursday?" To me he said, "The assignment was to describe someone you know well."

Three hands flew up, Tracy's among them. Shakespeare called on an older man, Mr. Bernstein. He stood up, and I could see his shoulders were hunched. He wore heavy glasses that slid partway down his nose, and before he began reading he shoved them up a bit. Nervously he shuffled his feet and cleared his throat. "This is about my dear wife, God rest her soul. I made it a poem. Okay?" Shakespeare simply nodded at him. Mr. Bernstein had a heavy accent that sounded vaguely familiar. Then it hit me; he sounded like Jacob. He cleared his throat again and began to read.

### "MY ANNA

"My Anna is a field of flowers hidden from all eyes,
  She is the dancing sunlight through which the
  sparrow flies.

"My Anna is the music that rises with the night,
  The melody of starshine, the hum of lunar light.

"Trampled by this century, murdered by brute force,
  Her heart retained its purity,
  Her soul has stayed the course."

Mr. Bernstein looked up from his paper and blinked. I could see tears standing in his eyes and felt them suddenly burning in my own. He sat down, and we all applauded. He blinked again and smiled.

"For Anna, a poem seemed the only way," he said with a shrug. "Her fiftieth *yahrzeit* is coming up this September. I'm going to ask the rabbi to read this if he will."

"What's *yahrzeit*?" Tracy asked.

"The time of year of her death. We Jews remember." He gave Tracy a sad smile.

"Fifty years ago?" Her voice held the wonder I felt.

"Ja. Come September. Fifty years dead. But never gone. Not to me."

"Nazis?" asked the woman sitting beside him.

He nodded yes and closed his eyes for a moment, then sighed. "So," he said, looking at Shakespeare, "you help me get the spelling right?"

"With pleasure, sir."

The next person to read was named Virginia. She was pale and thin, and her age was hard to guess, maybe twenty. Her dark yellow hair hung lankly at her shoulders, and she kept her mouth covered with one hand. I soon realized she was missing some teeth.

"Now, I got help with this," she started. "But you said that was all right. Is that right?" She had a twang that made her words bump into each other.

"It is," Shakespeare reassured her.

"This here is a description of my baby girl, Marvel."

I looked up in surprise. So this was Marvel's mother! I felt a thrill of connection.

"Marvel," she read, then never looked at the paper held tightly in her hand again. Instead she recited.

"Marvel is my daughter. She is twenty-two months old and weighs twenty-six pounds. She has a little curly blond hair, brown eyes, and the cutest cheeks you ever saw. She likes to blow bubbles out her mouth, which gets a little messy. She is patient and sweet. She has eight teeth and more coming. She is a marvel to me, which is why I named her that."

Again we all applauded. Virginia smiled with pleasure and quickly covered her mouth with her hand. "That's a good name for a baby," Mr. Bernstein told her. I wanted to tell her I knew Marvel, but I still felt too shy to speak.

Tracy was the last to read. She'd been chewing gum, which she took out of her mouth and delicately parked on her desktop. She stood up, and her eyebrows gathered in a frown as she stared at the paper she held. It was typed, I noticed.

"This is about my mother," she said, and glanced quickly at me. I smiled some encouragement her way and she began to read.

### "MY MOTHER

"Is my mother merely the typical everyday housewife she appears to be, or is she in fact a maniac? Hear me out and decide for yourself.

"Sally Sibowski, forty-two years old, stands five foot

two. She has very light blue eyes and wears pink lipstick, so her face is fairly colorful. She is the mother of four, of which I am the oldest. She's a member of the PTA, vice president of the Washco Democratic Club, and something like Bake Sale Specialist for the Firemen's Wives Auxiliary. Sounds pretty ordinary? But wait, there's more.

"She was born on April first, which she apparently took as a personal message on how to run her life. She has a totally primitive sense of humor and laughs at practically anything. Every year at Christmas she gives us something called the dumb-joke calendar, which is guaranteed to be worse than last year's. It always is, and she always loves it. Starts every day with a hoot, she says.

"To do housework, she turns the radio on full blast to this station that plays dinosaur music from the sixties or something, and goes around singing her head off and dancing with the vacuum cleaner. She uses a feather duster for a microphone and wails away like she's the original Elvis Presley. The last time I saw her do that, she started sneezing like crazy right in the middle of a song, and instead of getting discouraged she cracked up laughing. Hardly anything stops her.

"The other day, she and my little brother put cooking pots on their heads and wandered out in the yard with spoons, planting apple seeds. They were playing Johnny Appleseed. Anyway, the mailman stopped by when they were out there, and she chatted away with him, just like always, the pot on her head the whole time. She told me later she forgot it was there. Hmm.

"One more thing. She's some kind of whiz with numbers, and it wouldn't be fair to describe her and not mention this fact. She loves them—for all I know she dreams about them. I actually heard her say, and this is a direct quote, 'My idea of a good time is to sit down with a page of algebra.' Now that's the truth. Go figure. Her being good at math is fine, but she thinks all her children should be too. So far, none of us are, but we're holding out hopes for the baby. He can count up to three already, and he's not even one year old yet.

"When I was five, she started hypnotizing me at bedtime. At least that's what she *said* she was doing, although I doubt it because I remember everything. She was trying to 'teach arithmetic to my subconscious,' quote unquote, and she'd put me to sleep every night by making me take slow deep breaths and then saying the addition tables up to twelve. Same thing over and over—one plus one is two, one plus two is three. Up to twelve and back again. Eventually she went through not just addition but subtraction, multiplication, and division. Half the time I fell asleep in the middle of it, and if it worked, it's not very noticeable.

"I've included this little *antecdote* [here Tracy's eyebrows flew up, and I knew that this was a new word for her] because I think it says something important about her character. *What* it says, I'll leave to you to judge.

"I find it a bit embarrassing to go out with her in public, but my dad said I had to include in here that he doesn't.

"Which is true," Tracy said, looking up at the class for a moment. "They're going dancing tomorrow night, for instance." She rolled her eyes toward the ceiling, then continued to read.

"She chews one fingernail, loves red licorice the best, won't claim a favorite color, and drinks wine with dinner. She has a birthmark on her neck, which she persists in calling a beauty mark, but which is technically a dark brown spot the size of a dime that has been there since birth. She was born in Mercy Hospital and has lived on Washco all her life.

"So [Tracy glanced up at us] is Sally Sibowski the average housewife so many take her for? Or is she something more? Something less? You decide."

The class applauded loudly, and Tracy looked pleased. She sat down smiling broadly and popped her gum back into her mouth. "So you liked it, huh? Whaddya think?" she asked, looking at Shakespeare.

"I like the way you started it with a question," he said. "It got my attention."

"I thought it was great," I blurted out truthfully. I knew now something else we had in common—weird mothers.

"Well, good, good." Tracy was grinning away.

"And did you read this to your dear mother?" Mr. Bernstein asked.

"I did."

"And your mother? What did she say?"

"Just what you'd expect. She thought it was hysterical. Laughed like a hyena and said she was honored."

"You got a good mother," said the lady sitting next to Mr. Bernstein. "A little kooky? No harm. That keeps 'em young. You'll see. But what I want to know is how'd you make it so long? Mine came out short, and I tried to put everything in it."

Tracy shrugged. "I don't know. I just started writing, and by the time I got done it was long."

"Mrs. Dinsmore," Shakespeare said, "please don't compare yourself with others. We're all in different places, but we can learn from one another. Would you like to share yours?"

"No," she answered, and looked nervous. I felt nervous myself thinking he was going to make her.

But he didn't, merely smiled and said, "Maybe next time."

THE LAST HOUR was spent discussing books. This *was* different from school because everybody was reading something different. What surprised me most was that two people, Virginia and a man named Mr. Tson, were just learning how to read. Mr. Tson was from Cambodia, studying to become a United States citizen. He wanted to be able to read the Declaration of Independence by the end of the summer. He was a very quiet man who rarely spoke but who smiled at us, and he seemed to pay close attention to all that went on.

Virginia was hoping to learn enough so that she could read to Marvel. She (with Lucy, it turned out) had been working on *The Cat in the Hat*. "It's a page turner, all right," she said. "That cat is the devil! I swear. And I know this isn't reading, Mr. Oliver, but I think the pictures are real good."

"Look at the pictures all you want. That's part of it. I get pictures in my mind when I read."

"I do too," Mrs. Dinsmore said, "but I hate it when the picture on the cover doesn't match what's in my mind."

"I been getting ideas," Mr. Bernstein said. "Lots of them."

Shakespeare smiled. "Plato tends to do that to people."

"Ja. For many years I read Torah, I read newspapers, and that was that. Not since I was a schoolboy, long ago, have I read books." He pushed his thick glasses up a bit. "This Plato makes me think."

Tracy had just finished a biography of Harriet Tubman. "She was an awesome woman," she told us. "Incredible courage. I'm starting on Elizabeth Blackwell tonight." Tracy's goal, which I could hardly believe, was to read twenty biographies of famous people in two months.

"Twenty books in two months?" I asked in amazement.

"I'm a fast reader."

"And goals can be amended," Shakespeare added. "The first job is to set them."

Try as I might, I could think of no goal for myself.

Just as class was breaking up, Tracy's mother walked in. I didn't know who she was until Tracy said, "Hi, Ma." Mrs. Sibowski then made an elaborate curtsy (although she was wearing pants) and said, "Exhibit A. The maniac herself."

Everyone laughed, and Mr. Bernstein, who was standing, himself made a formal bow and said, "Madam, I salute you. A sense of humor is the lifesaver the Almighty tosses us when we've gone overboard."

True to his word, Shakespeare checked with me to see how I was getting home. Tracy's mother said she wanted to take me. I felt embarrassed at the number of "arrangements" that had to be made to get me a block and a half home, but then I noticed he checked with everyone in the class. Mr. Bernstein was walking Virginia back to the center. He lived just up the hill from there. Mrs. Dinsmore and Mr. Tson both had cars.

Our next writing assignment was to get a journal and "notice our life," as Shakespeare put it. "Do you have any questions?" he asked me as I was leaving. I couldn't think of any. "Any ideas for your reading?" I shook my head. "Okay. Maybe tomorrow, when I see you, we'll talk about it."

"Don't worry, Mr. Oliver," Tracy said, grabbing my arm. "I'll help her. Anything you need to know, you ask me. Got it?"

I nodded. "See ya," I said, letting Tracy pull me on.

"Yeah," she called back to him. "See you around like a doughnut."

Mrs. Sibowski made the usual motherly conversation. I found myself secretly watching her for signs of eccentricity, but none were too evident. "I'm so glad to meet you, Cab. I understand you're staying with your grandmother for the summer."

"Yes, ma'am."

"Ma'am," she repeated. "I haven't heard a child call a grown-up ma'am for twenty years. Those are awfully fine manners, but I hope you'll call me Sally from here on. Is that all right?"

"Yes, ma'am," I said automatically, and we all laughed.

She drove up a back alley and circled around to the top of Washco and then back down the cobblestone road in front of EATS. She pulled to the curb and let me out. "We'll wait till you get in. I hope to see you soon."

"You will, Mom," Tracy said, and squeezed my arm. As I was about to shut the door, she said, "Can I call you?"

"I guess so, but I don't know the number."

"Don't worry. See you tomorrow."

The lights were out in the restaurant. Tracy and her mother sat in the car while I fumbled with the key to the street door leading to our apartment. I felt intensely uncomfortable knowing they were watching me, as though they would like me less now that I was keeping them waiting. Naturally, because I was trying not to be, I got clumsy and it took a while before I could get the key to turn. Finally it did, and I waved good-bye, went in, and shut the door behind me.

For a few moments I just stood there at the bottom of the steps, slumped against the door, resting. Images of the day washed over me. What a long one! And full. I saw Mr. Bernstein's face as he read his poem, saw Mr. Tson nodding and smiling, got a flash of Mrs. Dinsmore's perfume. I remembered the twang in Virginia's voice and the discovery that here was Marvel's mother. I saw Shakespeare looking serious. And at the center of all the images spinning through my mind stood Tracy. At the library, upstairs in my room, meeting Jessica and Bill, in the car with her mother. Tracy.

It seemed a long time from morning, when I had walked up to buy flowers for Mr. Johansson. Longer still since the night before, when Mac had barged in on me doing dishes.

Meeting Tracy changed everything for me on Washco. It was like meeting another self. A real friend. I wondered if Gretchen would be jealous, but figured she'd probably understand, would maybe even think it showed "good adjustment." Tracy and I were different. She was a lot more outgoing, flamboyant, and seemed at ease with people. I thought of her conviction of Greatness and knew she was more ambitious. But beneath all that, I had the sense that in some way we were just alike, as though a part of me had been there, growing up on Washco all along, and now we'd met and could commence being friends.

Standing in the dim yellow light of the hall, I felt a part of Washco. As though I belonged.

GRANDMOTHER WAS SITTING in her room, deep in her battered armchair, feet soaking in a pan of hot water and Epsom salts. She did this every night to "ease her dogs."

"So whaddya know?" she asked when I poked my head in.

"Whew," I said. "It's more than I can explain. I have to get a journal and write things down. You ever heard of that?"

"Hmm."

"Bill's not home?"

"No." Her eyes sparkled a bit. "He's at the movies, if you catch my meaning."

"Jessica?"

She nodded. "Tell me," she asked, and I was thrilled at the conspiratorial tone of her voice, "is Bill the type to be easily smitten?"

"Smitten?"

"Uh, taken with a girl. The way he is with Jess."

I thought about it. "Well, he had a girlfriend for a while, but they broke up last year. Nobody since then very steady." After a minute I asked, "So you think this might be serious?"

"Wouldn't be surprised. I see signs."

For a while we discussed the "signs" and agreed to watch for more. She too had noticed the small smiles, and the way they looked at each other—"google-eyed" was her term. For an old woman my grandmother had a keen interest in young love. At least as far as Bill was concerned.

It was easy for me to understand how someone might fall in love with Bill. And having met Jessica, I could well imagine she wasn't too hard to care about herself.

That night, when I woke to the sound of a bottle breaking on the street below, I merely pulled the sheet higher and nestled in, thinking, Oh, Washco.

# eleven

Mr. Johansson came home in a taxi the next day. As promised, I took a tray of food to him at lunch. Grandmother had sent vegetable soup, rolls, a thermos of coffee, and lemon pie. His apartment, unlike ours, was not above but in the back of his shop. I stood peering into the front window, trying to figure out how to knock while holding the tray, when Hannah opened the door.

"That man is bad!" she said to me by way of greeting.

"What's wrong?" I asked.

"Maybe food will put him in his right mind," she said, but eyed the tray dubiously.

We walked through the long, narrow shop. His place was dark and crowded. A long counter contained shoes of every imaginable variety, in pairs and alone; lathes, shoehorns, strips of leather, a tap hammer, coffee cans growing unknown species of houseplants, and a large ancient black cash register with a donation box for crippled children beside it. What I liked best about his shop was the smell, oil and leather mixed with something else I can't name, something sharp and strong.

Hannah held the door for me, and I walked through. With a shock I realized his apartment was the size of our kitchen at EATS. The space had been divided into two rooms, a kitchen and a bedroom. Both were very small. To my surprise Mr. Johansson was sitting at the kitchen table. I'd imagined he'd be in bed, especially after hearing he was "bad."

His head was wrapped in white bandages, and his face looked very gray in contrast, but he smiled when he saw me. "So, the little one comes to see me. Thank you, child."

"Grandmother says for you not to worry about food," I told him, setting down the tray. Covertly I studied him. He actually seemed better than I'd feared.

"Your grandmother is a good soul. You tell her I say thank you. With her food inside me, I'll soon be back at work. Now you, sit. Visit with an old man. Yes?" I sat.

Slowly he set about eating, and I realized that chewing was painful for him. I felt a wave of tremendous hurt rise in me. I knew he was in pain, could feel it clearly for myself, although he said nothing of it.

At last he pushed back the tray. He had not eaten much. He looked at both Hannah and me as we sat across from him at his tiny table. He tapped the table with one long finger and said solemnly, "Something has got to be done."

Hannah sighed and pursed her mouth.

"About what?" I asked, feeling lost.

"About these streets." His tone was resolved, determined, very plain.

"They caught the guy who . . . who did this to you," I offered.

"Yes. They caught one. But that's no good. He'll be back at it tonight." His words echoed Mac's from the day before. His finger continued to tap. "Something has got to be done," he said again, this time tapping out each word.

"And you're the old fool who thinks he's got to do it," Hannah said scornfully. "What'd he do to you? Knock a screw loose in there?"

Mr. Johansson smiled at her. "He knocked some sense into me is what he did. Some sense. This can't go on. It's got to stop."

She rose from her chair and looked out the window. All I could see was the kerchiefed back of her head, but I could hear her muttering to herself.

"How?" I asked Mr. J. "How are you going to stop it?"

He sighed. "Now that I don't know. Not yet. But nonetheless—it's got to stop." He glanced at Hannah. "No one should live like this, afraid to go out on the street. Yes?"

I agreed with him. "I'll help."

Suddenly Hannah whirled around and descended on me. "Oh, no, you don't, young lady. And you either, old man. Putting ideas in a young girl's head. You ought to be ashamed. We got police to see to this sort of thing. Mac caught him, didn't he? Can't you be satisfied with that?"

He merely looked at her, sadly, and made no answer.

"No wars on Washco," she said harshly. Then to me, "You understand?"

"Yes, ma'am." I had been surprised by her fierceness, yet oddly aware that although she sounded angry, what she really felt was scared.

"Relax, Hannerl." He spoke to her in a calm, gentle voice. "I won't make a war. I'll make a peace, yes? Those hooligans, they're the ones making war. We've got to do something. Try not to worry so."

"I don't like seeing you like this," Hannah said, gesturing toward him. "Look at you, for God's sake. You're wounded."

"I understand," he said softly, and there passed between them a look that excluded me completely.

He had me make a sign for his front window before I left. Temporarily Closed. Please Call Again. I wrote it for him on the back of a brown paper bag, as that was all we could find for sign making. But I was going to the drugstore that afternoon with Tracy to get my journal (she had called early, my first phone call at EATS) and I offered to get him some white poster board to redo it on. "It will show up better," I told him, and he agreed.

Tracy and I met at the corner at two o'clock and walked to the drugstore. We browsed the makeup and jewelry aisle and made our way to the stationery. She showed me the kind of book she used for a journal, a black bound composition book.

"What do you do if you make mistakes?" I asked, as it was the type you couldn't easily pull pages out of.

"I just cross them out and go on," she said. "It's a journal. You're allowed to make all the mistakes you want."

I nodded and thought again of my mother's diary; her slanting handwriting had many crossed-out places. But she hadn't known anyone else would read it. She had thought it was private. This journal, however, was supposed to be turned in from time to time. Shakespeare would read whatever I wrote. That thought gave me pause. I finally picked a plain spiral notebook, not too big.

Tracy assured me she had just the right materials at home for making Mr. J.'s sign. We had decided to go to her house until four o'clock, when I had to get back to work. She lived just a few blocks away.

Her street was lined with trees, and all of the houses had long, sloping lawns. The sight reminded me of Mom's apple tree. Tracy's house was big— three stories of red brick with a huge, messy front

*114*

porch. Sitting on the steps were two redheaded twins, a boy and a girl, about seven years old. They were armed with water pistols and squirted us as we approached. "Sprout and Doubt," Tracy said by way of introduction. "They drive me crazy, if you know what I mean."

"Well, I don't really," I replied, thinking of Bill. "But I believe you," I added, wiping water from my face.

Sally was in the kitchen and called us to come say hello. She offered lemonade, which I accepted gratefully. "This is Sam," Tracy said, pointing out the baby who sat on the floor pulling things out of a cabinet.

"Now, Trace, just watch what he's doing for a minute," Sally said. And so we did. Sam was busily reaching in for more plastic bowls, lids, and a host of other junk. He had a huge pile beside him and was adding to it. "I really do think he's counting," Sally said after we'd watched.

"I sincerely hope so, Mom. For all our sakes," Tracy answered with a grin.

We went upstairs to Tracy's room, which was on the third floor. It was a big room, light and colorful and jammed full of things. I was surprised to find she had a double bed. Somehow I'd assumed that all kids had singles, or a bunk bed at most. Hers was unmade and strewn, like most of the room, with clothes. On all the walls hung posters and pictures of horses.

Along one wall was a long table covered with books, papers, a typewriter, a globe, a lamp, and odds and ends beyond counting. From this seeming chaos she pulled a neat rectangle of white poster board and a handful of colored markers. We lettered the sign carefully, and I added a drawing of a shoe in one corner, which Tracy loyally admired.

Mr. Johansson admired it too that evening when I delivered it, along with his supper. "That PLEASE CALL AGAIN is just right," he said. "And most important. I *will* be back, you know. This is not the end of me."

"Pish, old man," Hannah scolded. "Who said it was? But for now you need rest. *Bed rest.* Get better, then you can start the revolution." It seemed to me their squabble had continued since morning, yet neither of them seemed upset.

I managed to avoid Shakespeare that day, which I did out of guilt. I hadn't gotten my library card or set a goal. I was in the class mostly because Tracy wanted me there. It didn't look that bad from what I had seen the night before, but I was still leery of being educated during the summer.

Eventually, though, I did break down and choose a book, *Jane Eyre*. Don't ask me why. It seemed like a challenge (and I was right about that), but in a way, its very thickness looked like it might provide protection. I knew it was famous, and I could tell just by leafing through it was hard.

*116*

When I told Shakespeare my pick, he only nodded and asked, "What's your goal?"

"To read it," I replied irritably, as though that was self-evident, which it was, to me.

"Let me know what you think" was all he said.

Little did I expect to actually enjoy the book, but I did. Jane Eyre was so badly treated, so scorned by adults, and so misunderstood that I felt a sympathy for her that made it possible to keep plowing through the parts I didn't understand. She was also spunky and tough, which I admired, and she got in so much trouble it was hard not to like her.

The writing was harder, but I kept at it. Since no one ever had to read if they didn't want to, I never volunteered. I enjoyed listening to the others, and found to my surprise that I even enjoyed "noticing my life" in my journal.

The hardest part about it was manners. To write something down was to notice it practically out loud. And it seemed to me I had an eye for noticing things I'd been taught not to mention. Like nose hairs or bad breath. I tried to explain this once in my journal and Shakespeare wrote me back in his crabby little script, "Notice away. In your journal you write what you want."

WITHIN A WEEK Mr. Johansson was back behind his counter mending shoes. He never stood quite as tall as he did before he was mugged, but almost. For a while he was dizzy a lot and used a cane to get around. The back of his head—once the bandages came off—was ugly looking. The stitches were black, the hair had been shaved and grew in white and stubby, and even after the stitches came out, the scar gaped red and raw.

He and I became friends. I fell into the habit of visiting him the two weeks I brought him his meals, and even after I would stop by sometimes just to say hello. He would always say, "I'm still working on it. Don't you worry." And I didn't. I couldn't imagine what he would come up with to make the streets of Washco safer, but I had a profound faith that he would think of something.

One time I found him sitting on the floor in his bedroom, surrounded by towers of books, like a maze. "The scholars," he said, gesturing to the stacks. "They all know so much, but they don't know what I want to know."

"And what's that?" I asked, joining him on the floor inside his dusty castle.

"How to stop the sons of—the creeps," he amended for my benefit. "The no-goodniks, as your grand-father used to call them."

"No-goodniks?" I laughed. "He really called people that? No-goodniks?" I added this little pebble of information to the few others I had about Oscar Doyle.

"Oh, yes. The ruling class, management, and

scabs of course. Well, scabs he called worse. Who wouldn't?"

"What are scabs?" I knew vaguely, but I wasn't sure.

"People who try to break a strike, who'll walk right through a union picket line. Garbage." He made a spitting sound to show his disgust.

Hannah was often over there too, or sometimes I would find him sunk in one of the upholstered rocking chairs in her junk store, the two of them invariably arguing, but never bitterly. At least not when I was around.

And so it was a month passed. Since finding Tracy, I was much happier. I still worried about the future, but she worried about it with me, which was some consolation. My days had a sort of pattern to them: working in the morning, seeing Tracy in the afternoon and maybe going by the center, seeing Lucy or taking Marvel to the playground, maybe Mr. J., then more work, and dinner, and Bill coming home, and lots of times, most days, Jessica with him. Then at night I'd call Tracy, or she would call me, and we'd catch up or just talk. Tuesdays and Thursdays we had class, and most nights, before I went to bed, I did my noticing in my journal. We had a few letters from Mom, more gush as far as I could tell, but I hadn't really missed her much, which I counted to my credit.

# *twelve*

THEN CAME THE TIME—we had been there exactly a month—when the telephone rang in the middle of the night. I heard it and jerked awake, worried at once, as what could it be but bad news? I heard Bill's big feet hit the floor in his room down the hall, heard him fumbling around, and finally heard him answer it. And then there went through me a stab of cold terror. His voice was wrong. All wrong. "What?" he said, and "Where?" and then, "I'll be right there." Each word hit the floor like a stone.

I sat up and heard him slam down the receiver. And then, worst of all, I heard him make a sound I had never heard from Bill, not in all our years— like a sick cat he moaned, and the very air was full of anguish. Then he was moving back toward his room, and I was up and after him.

"Bill," I called softly, opening his door and trying to focus my eyes. "What's wrong?"

He turned around and stared at me as though he had never seen me before, didn't know me. It made me sick. His hair was stuck in funny angles from where he'd been sleeping, and his eyes looked wild, crazy. I had never seen him look like that and I was badly scared. He even walked over to me, but was looking out the door, not at me. "Bill." I tugged at his sleeve. "Please tell me what's wrong."

It was the tug that got his attention. He saw me then and looked right at me. I felt myself drawing back, there was something so awful in his look. Then he shut those terrible eyes and pressed his hands to them. Another moan escaped, and he put his hand out, whether to draw me near or keep me away I don't know. "Cab," he said at last. "It's Jessica."

"What, Bill? What?" But by then I didn't really want to know. I was too afraid of his answer.

But he didn't answer, not immediately. He shook his head. "She's at the hospital. I'm going there now."

"Bill, what is it?"

He looked at me then as though he hated me and spoke in a hard voice I'd never heard before. "She was raped, Cab. Raped. Now get out of here. I have to go."

I felt as if he had punched me in the stomach. I stood where he pushed me, out in the dark hall, my feet gripping the cold linoleum, shivering.

In less than a minute he came out of his room, barged right into me as though I wasn't there, but

I was, and he knew it, for he said, "Tell Gran," and was gone, running down the steps. I just stood there, shivering, listening until I heard the car engine start and then the squeal of tires as Bill pulled out of the alley.

Grandmother called out, "Bill? Bill?" She sounded very old and croaky. I opened her door, and she said, "Bill, is that you?"

"No," I answered, and I sounded croaky myself. "It's Cab."

I climbed into bed with her, something I had never done before. Her bed was warm and soft and smelled of lavender. She pulled the sheets around me. "Did you have a bad dream, love?" she asked. I knew then she hadn't heard the phone.

"No," I said, and started to cry. This was worse than a bad dream, I thought. It was real. I, who cry rarely, could not stop myself then. My stomach hurt badly, as though Bill really had punched me, and sobbing hurt it more, but I couldn't stop. Finally, I was able to say the words, the same ones Bill had said to me, "Jessica was raped."

"Oh. No," my grandmother cried out, and then slumped back in bed and pulled me closer. "Oh, no," she said over and over, softer now. "Oh, no," patting me on the back. "Oh, no." Just that: "Oh. No."

We passed what remained of that night in tears and holding, little sleep, and soft talk. In the morning we began to wait. For Bill, for word, for whatever it was that would come next.

At five, Grandmother got up. She ran a dry, wrinkled hand across my forehead and whispered, "You sleep."

"No," I cried, desperately afraid to be alone. I too got up, stumbling with tiredness and the burden of it all. I knew what the word *rape* meant—forced sex. But what I didn't know, and was afraid to lie in bed and wonder about, was what rape would mean for Jessica, Bill's beautiful Jess of the laughing eyes, the burnt-honey voice, the shining hair.

I had seen Bill and Jessica kissing not three days before. They were on the back stoop, coming up from the alley where Bill always parked. I was in the kitchen getting ready to take the garbage out and saw them just as I was fixing to open the door. Like the spy that I am, I put the garbage down and watched them get out of the car. Bill came around and put his arm around her waist. He said something to her, and she laughed and looked up at him, snuggling her head into his neck. And then they kissed.

Kissing, at least at that time in my life, fell into much the same category as car accidents we passed on the highway. I both did and didn't want to look. They didn't kiss long, but long enough for Bill to draw his arms tightly around her, for Jessica to throw her arms up around his neck and lean her own head way back. And when they finished, they continued to stand there, looking at each other. Bill ran his hand through her hair, separating it and letting light fall through the auburn strands. Jessica was looking at Bill, and I couldn't see her face, but I could see Bill's. I knew for certain this was one of the signs Grandmother had told me to watch for. Bill was in love.

I dressed quickly and was turned, ready to go downstairs, when I saw my journal sitting on the desk where I'd left it the night before. I took my pencil and wrote the words "Jessica was raped last night." I stared at what I'd written and tried, seeing it in writing, to understand it. But I couldn't. That one sentence seemed to loom at me, meaning so much and yet just words. I added the date, shut the book, and went down to join Grandmother in the long day ahead.

Mac was in early as usual and told us what he knew, which was what was in the police report. Jessica had been working at the Centralia, and she got off at midnight. Her car was parked, as it was always, across the street, beside the high school. There was a parking lot in the back alley for theater employees, Mac told us, but she didn't use it. The alley was too dark, whereas Washco, the front street, stayed lit. He shook his head and went on.

She was leaving work, unlocking her car, when a man came up from behind and grabbed her. She screamed and he punched her. In the face. The force of it knocked her down, and he yanked her up by the arm and punched her again. He dragged her up the steps of the school and into the yard. There he stole her money and then raped her. When he left, she grabbed her clothes and ran back to the street. Ran to the fire station, which is just up the block. The men there called the medics, of course, and the police.

Mac's voice was weary with the telling of this awful tale. Before he began, he'd told Grandmother perhaps I should not hear it. She shook her head, said, "Cab lives here too," and stood with an arm around me the whole time he talked. I felt shudders go through her as his story unfolded and leaned in closer, though to comfort her or myself I don't know.

When he finished, we were silent. Then Grandmother made a whimpering sound, high and mournful. "Oh, Michael," she said, and her voice, usually so gruff and full, sounded reedy and thin, as though it might break. "That dear girl. That poor little girl. What's it come to, Michael, can you tell me that?"

Mac made no answer.

"I'd better keep working," she said with a sigh. "Or I'll take to my bed and not want to get up."

Again I felt close to tears and turned away.

"We'll do our best to catch him. You know that, Maddie."

She only nodded.

Like all news on Washco, this traveled fast. Mrs. Mondelli had already heard when she stopped in, for once at a loss for words. She and my grandmother stared mutely at each other, shaking their heads. Hannah clasped her hand to her chest and gasped for breath when Grandmother told her. "Oh, my God!" she cried. "And what next? Is there no end to it? Aah."

I myself told Mr. Johansson. I knocked on his back door, as I knew his shop wasn't open yet. He pulled the door wide and regarded me solemnly. "Last night, I saw the boy. Your brother, yes?"

"Bill," I said, and shut my eyes against the memory of his face as I'd last seen it.

"An old man. I don't sleep much. Come, child, sit down." Kindly he guided me to a kitchen chair and sat next to me. He didn't rush me, but sat and waited.

And finally, not meeting his eyes, I got the story out. He bore the news quietly. We both stared at the table. "Some men," he said finally, "some men are animals. Enough is enough. Something has got to be done."

"But what?" I asked him, and knew I sounded accusing. "What?" I asked again, gripped suddenly by rage. I realized then that I'd wanted to be the one to tell him because in some way I blamed him. *Him*. Mr. Johansson. I felt my face contort with anger, heard my voice go strange. "You promised you'd think of something. You promised." Even as I was shouting at him, I knew I was being unfair, knew it wasn't his fault he hadn't figured out a way to stop crime on Washco. But it felt good, in an awful way it felt wonderful, to shout.

"Leave me alone," he said. "I have to think."

"Think?" I yelled. "Is that all you can do is think?"

He looked at me strangely then. "Yes," he said quietly. "That's all I can do. But you, you can get angry, and that is good too, yes? Now go."

I slammed his back door on my way out for good measure. But in the chill morning air my anger drained from me like water from a sieve. I was left with a shaky weakness, a trembling that seemed to come from my very blood.

Tracy, her mother, the twins, and Sam all came in that morning. Sally and Grandmother greeted each other warmly, but with such seriousness I knew she'd already heard about Jessica. Tracy's eyebrows were drawn in pain and question, and as I was busy waiting tables, we had time for nothing more than a look. They took the middle booth, and Sally ordered pancakes all around. The twins were bouncing with excitement, and as soon as they'd eaten she sent them to the library playground to run off some energy, and sent Tracy to keep an eye on them.

Grandmother went to Sally then and put her hand on her shoulder. I too went to their booth and sat down, exhausted. "Maddie," Sally said, looking up at my grandmother, "I'm calling a meeting."

"A meeting?"

"Yes. You know. Everyone. Get everyone who

lives here together. We've got to talk about what is going on. It's becoming unlivable. And this is our home."

"A meeting?" Grandmother asked this again as though she had never heard of a meeting.

"Maddie. We've got to do something."

"Yes."

"I have daughters. You do too. And grands." She looked at me and smiled. I smiled back.

"Okay," Grandmother said abruptly. "Here?"

"Yes, that's what I thought," Sally said.

"You think it's big enough?"

"For a start. Oh, Maddie, let's start. This is horrible." Her voice had risen in pitch, and Sam, who was sitting on her lap, reached up for her cheek.

"When?" Grandmother asked.

"The sooner the better. Tonight? Tomorrow?"

"Tomorrow's Friday. That's as good as any."

"Seven?"

"Done."

What was decided by them was carried out by Tracy and me. Sally wrote out a flier that read STOP CRIME. ALL CITIZENS INVITED. EATS at 7:00 P.M. FRIDAY. Tracy and I got them copied for free on the machine at the library.

We walked Washco that afternoon, delivering them to store owners, who put them in their windows. We tacked them on doors, on telephone poles, on anything we could find. By five o'clock the hill was covered. I hadn't been able to give one to Mr.

Johansson. I gave two to Hannah instead, and asked her to deliver it. She agreed but looked at me so long I knew he'd told her about my temper that morning. I hurried away. Shakespeare passed the fliers out in class that night and encouraged people to come. I was so tired by then that I have no memory of what else, if anything, happened.

And all that day there was no Bill, and no word of him either. But when he finally did come home that night, I wished he hadn't. I was in the kitchen, just home from class and getting a snack, when he came in. He was all shoulder and elbow, passing through in a hurry without a word. He had his face turned down, and I couldn't see him, only a glimpse of his hair and the set of his chin as he ran up the steps and slammed the door to his room. This from Bill.

Tired as I was, I went into Grandmother's room before I went to bed. She was soaking her feet; I sat on the bed. "Is this why Mom left?" I asked her.

"Beg your pardon?"

"Is this why my mother left Washco? Because it was so . . . so dangerous? Is that why?"

"Whatever gave you that idea?" she asked, looking at me sharply.

"Nothing gave it to me," I answered back, sharp myself. "I just wondered." Did Grandmother know about the word HELP on Mom's old desk? "It's not like this in Blue Cloud. I mean, there's crime, I guess." I couldn't really think of any. "But not like this. You can walk around at night and not think about it. At least we always did."

"Well, that's a fine thing," Grandmother said. "I hope they never lose it. It's exactly what we're needing back here. And ain't got. The safety. The feeling of security we used to have. As a neighborhood." She shook her head slowly, and I saw her mouth twitch. "No, dear. I doubt very much if your mother left Washco because of the danger. Unless it wasn't dangerous *enough* for her back then. Washco was pretty tame twenty years ago. A tolerably civilized place."

"So what happened?"

She shrugged. "Everyone has their theories. There's a lot of unemployment, but then there's jobs go begging, so it's hard to say. Part of it's drugs, no doubt. This cocaine and crack and what all. I suppose if you're addicted you might do horrible things to get money. Not to mention what people do when they're high. I don't really know. That's the bottom line, dear. I don't know."

I listened and thought about it. I'd heard it all before. "But what about rape?" I asked it fast and in a whisper.

She sighed and stirred her feet in the steaming tub. "Some people are sick, Cab. Twisted." I looked up and stared. It was exactly what Mom had told me years ago about child abuse. "They *want* to hurt other people," she continued. "It's bad. I won't tell you a lie. But," and here she caught her breath and looked around the room, "I really think most people—for the most part, now—most people are good."

That night I checked on the moon. What was it Bill had told me? It was the same moon shining on us all? Was it shining on Jessica that night? And my mother? Did the moon shine over Rome, I think it was, that week? And Gretchen home in Blue Cloud? Could she see it? And Bill? There was no sound at all from his room. He who was closest seemed farthest away.

# *thirteen*

B ILL WAS GONE in the morning by the time I got up. Grandmother said she wanted Tracy and me to run some errands for her. Jessica was at home and would be in bed for a while. "She's pretty beat up" is the way Grandmother put it. She wanted us to deliver some food, and Tracy would know the way.

Our first stop was at the center. Sally had a list of names and phone numbers for Lucy. They were both spending the day on the phone, rounding up people for the meeting that night. Lucy was watching for us and met us at the door. Her face was pale, and she had dark circles under her eyes. She thanked us for the list and invited us to wait until the weather cleared. It had begun to spit rain as it seems to me it did so often that summer.

"No, some of this food is hot," I said, indicating the covered tray I carried. "And Grandmother said she wanted it to be that way when we got there, so I 'spect we better be off. Right, Trace?"

"Right, podner," she said, in what she considered a west Texas accent.

"Say hey to Marvel for me," I said.

"Will do. I think you'll see her tonight. And girls?" Lucy turned and walked to her desk, where she picked up a bundle of long-stem flowers, some of them still buds. "Will you give these to Jess?" She handed them to Tracy.

"What are they?" I asked.

"Gladiola." Lucy gazed at the pink and orange flowers rather sadly. "If you see her. Jess, I mean. Give her my love."

We both nodded and left.

Neither one of us spoke as we cut through the alley and up toward Washco. Lucy's somber mood had washed off on us. I had begun to worry about seeing Jessica. What would she look like? What should I say?

When we walked past the high school, Tracy said, "Right here is where he grabbed her." I shuddered in the rain and kept walking, looking not at the street, not at the school, not at anything but the covered tray I was carrying.

"They haven't caught him, you know," she said in a low voice. I knew. I'd heard the same from Mac a few hours earlier. We walked on.

"Tracy, how could it happen so close to the fire station?"

She looked at me. "According to my dad, it can happen anywhere, day or night. That's what he said. Nobody heard her scream. But she only screamed once before she got—hit. Maybe it wasn't very loud."

"Oh, God. I feel sick." I was suddenly afraid I might vomit, right there on the street.

"Turn up here," Tracy said. "We still have two blocks to go. Don't give out on me, okay?"

"Okay."

The street we turned onto was crowded with row houses, jammed together on the side of the hill. I realized we were only a block over from where Tracy lived. Jessica's house was indistinguishable from her neighbors'. We climbed the steps in dripping silence and knocked on the door. It was answered almost immediately, much to my surprise, by Bill.

"What do you want?" he asked, and it sounded like a growl.

"Grandmother sent food," I told him, and tried to catch his eye. He turned away. His eyes were slits and darting.

"Well, let us in, for pete's sake," Tracy said. "We're soaking."

"I know you are, and I don't want you dripping all over the house." Still, he stood back enough for us to come into the foyer. Bill took the food and the flowers into the kitchen. "Stay where you are," he ordered.

*134*

I heard voices, and in a moment Bill was back, an older man with him. I felt Tracy stiffen.

"This is Mr. Hawkins," Bill said to me. "Jessica's father. This is my sister, Cab. You know Tracy."

"Yes, I do. Thanks for the grub." He reached out and shook hands with me. I noticed his was shaking ever so slightly, like a palsy. He was a short man, only a little taller than me. "Tell Mrs. Doyle thank you for us. Jess is sleeping," he said, and glanced toward the steps. "I'll tell her you came by."

"Okay, let's go," Tracy said. I could feel her impatience to be out of there. I too wanted to leave, but I wanted Bill to look at me first, just once. He didn't, merely pushed me none too gently toward the door.

"Bill," I said.

"Go on." His tone was softer, but he still wouldn't meet my eye.

Outside, we pulled the hoods of our raincoats up again and started down the steps. I looked back at the house, but the door had closed, the blinds were drawn. No one watched us leave.

"So what is it?" I asked Tracy, referring to her evident dislike of Mr. Hawkins.

"He's a souse," she said shortly.

"A souse?"

"Yeah, you know, an alky, a drunk. He's a bum is what he is. I hate him." I had sensed that. "What do you call them in Texas?"

"Well, my mother calls them al-co-hol-ics." I used her careful phrasing. "But of course she's a social worker." I laughed. As if that explained something.

"Well, whatever, that's what he is. He drinks."

"Where's her mom?"

"She died a long time ago. Supposedly"—and here Tracy turned to me, her eyebrows up, clearly expressing doubt—"that's why he drinks."

"Oh."

I felt confused. Somehow, in the weeks that I'd known Jessica, it never occurred to me she came from a family that was just her and her alcoholic father. I'd imagined a big family for her, something like Tracy's. Not this.

"They're backward," Tracy said, and I had a momentary vision of Jessica and her father walking backward around their house.

"What do you mean?"

"It's like he's the child and she's the mother. I've known Jess all my life. Even when she was just a kid, it was like she took care of him. You know, cooking, doing the laundry—all that stuff. She probably signed her own report cards. Mom says he's pathetic, that's her word. I call it gross. Supposedly, he can't help himself. It's a sickness."

"He seemed sober enough just now."

"Oh, yeah. He's probably holding out as long as he can. You notice how his hands were shaking?"

"Yes."

"Well, pretty soon he's going to go get a drink or

two, and trust me, nobody will see him again for three or four days. That's the way it always goes."

"Yuck."

"Really."

We were walking to Tracy's house. Sally must have been watching for us, as she met us on the front porch. "You girls are soaked. Come on in," she said, and took our jackets. "How about some tea? With honey?" She steered us into the kitchen and busied herself at the stove, but only for a moment.

"You know, I 've been thinking," she said, joining us at the table.

"Oh, Mom. You know how dangerous that can be," Tracy said jokingly.

"I know," she answered with a sigh, completely ignoring or missing the joke. "But I can't help it." I realized then it was more than her tone that was serious; her whole body looked tired, sagging. Tracy was right about her mother loving to joke around, but there was nothing playful about her just then. "I think rape"—she glanced to each of us—"is truly a horrible crime. Horrible. And it's something nobody much wants to talk about. I know I don't. But here's what I want to say to you two, both of you," and she looked from Tracy to me, eye to eye. "If you have any questions about it, either what happened to Jessica, or well, about any of it . . . I . . . well, please ask. I might not know the answer, but I might. And it's better than wondering about it by yourself. Okay?"

"Okay, Mom. I promise," Tracy said.

"Cab? I know this isn't really my place, but with your mother gone . . ." She didn't finish her sentence. I could sense her discomfort.

"It's okay," I told her. "My mother would say just the same if she were here. Any questions, and all that. She always says that." Sally smiled at me gently, and I smiled back a little.

Suddenly the kettle whistled, and she got up to pour the tea. "Mom," Tracy said to her back.

"Uhm?"

"Is she going to get, you know, pregnant?"

"No," Sally said. "When they took her to the hospital, they gave her something called the 'morning-after pill.' It's a huge dose of some kind of hormone. It'll probably start her period, and make her kind of nauseated, but she won't be pregnant."

I stirred my tea, added more honey. "Is she going to be okay?" I asked, avoiding her eye.

Sally didn't answer, so I did look up, and saw she was looking at me with huge blue eyes spilling over with tears. I looked away. "I don't know, Cab. I just don't know. I hope to God so, but only time will tell. You'll have to excuse me. I've been crying over this for two days. Jess is like my own girl." Her voice broke then, and she cried a little harder, wiping her face with her hand. I could feel tears stinging again in my own eyes and swallowed them back.

"Do you think they're going to catch him?" Tracy asked.

"Let's hope so. Apparently she gave the police a pretty good description, so maybe."

"Maybe," Tracy echoed.

"I think I hear Sam," Sally said. Then, smiling again, she went on, "Shortest napper in the East. Can you stay for lunch, Cab?"

"I better get back." Mostly I just wanted to be by myself for a while. "See you tonight."

The rain had let up, which is not to say the sun had come out. It was as gray a day as any I'd seen. I kept my head tucked down as I passed Mr. Johansson's, but it was Hannah who waylaid me. She'd been standing in the doorway of her shop and called to me as I hurried by. "Hello," she said, flashing her gold tooth as she smiled. "What's your hurry? Come here. I have something to show you."

I paused, trying to be polite, but aggravated. I wasn't in the mood for her crystal ball. "I can't right now," I said. "I'm supposed to be back." This was an out-and-out lie. Grandmother had told me to take my time.

"Come on, this won't take a minute. And you'll be glad you did."

I went in and let my eyes adjust to the dim, dusty light. Her shop was laden with junk. Dressers, tables, chairs, chests, lamps, stools, toasters, and televisions were stacked everywhere. Lamp shades hung from the ceiling, and in one corner there were clothes hanging and others piled in a heap. She led me toward the rack of clothes and parted it. There, on the floor, tucked back a ways, was a blanket, and on it her gray cat, Bella, and five mewling kittens. They were newborn, still slick from their birth. Squeaking and eyes shut, they sought their mother's milk.

"Oh." I fell to my knees to see them closer. "They're beautiful." This was a bit of an exaggeration, but I was fascinated.

"I thought you'd like to see them," Hannah said with satisfaction. "Just born."

"So life goes on, I see."

I jumped, hearing Mr. Johansson's deep voice. He was standing behind me, near Hannah. I shot her as dirty a look as I dared, knowing somehow that she had contrived this meeting.

I stood up and let the clothes fall back to hide Bella's treasure.

"So how are you?" he asked rather pointedly.

"Fine," I mumbled. "But I've got to go." I stared at his nobbly collarbone.

"Of course. A lot to do to get ready for tonight, yes?"

"Yes. Are you coming?" I asked timidly.

"Oh, yes. I'll be there."

"Wild horses couldn't keep this one away." Hannah laughed. "He'll be there for sure, you can count on that."

"So will I," I said rather stupidly, but I was trying to make some kind of a truce.

"Yes. Tonight we have a meeting. This is good, yes?" I could tell he was trying too.

"Oh, I know you." Hannah poked him in his ribs with her stout finger. "A chance to tell them all how it's because of the capitalists running everything."

"Well, it's only the truth, Hannerl." He sounded a little hurt.

"So maybe it is," she snapped. "I'm not saying it's not. But what are we going to do about it now? Here. Today. Tonight. We can't wait for the revolution. What are we going to do now? That's the question, my philosophical friend. Not who caused it, or who's to blame. But what to do."

"The question is very much on my mind as well," he said, and looked at me. "I *have* been thinking."

I looked away. "Gotta go," I tossed behind me, before either one of them could say any more. "See you tonight."

"Tonight," they both called to me as I left. Tonight.

# *fourteen*

EATS WAS PACKED BY SEVEN. There
was no more room for people to sit, so many stood.
I was kept busy serving coffee and soft drinks and
didn't bother to count, but we were past full. I realized that I knew almost everyone there, either because they were regulars or because I'd seen them
around the neighborhood. Jessica didn't come, and
neither did Bill. But Mr. Bernstein, whom I knew
from class, did. So did Mr. Tson. He stood crammed
in a corner, nodding and smiling, his face drawn and
serious, even through the smile.

And Lucy came, and Virginia, Marvel, and several
others from the center whom I knew by sight, if not
by name. The back booth was taken over by children, and Tracy was in charge of them: the twins,
Sam, Marvel, another little girl from the center I
hadn't met. Except for that booth the majority of
heads in the restaurant were gray.

Grandmother rang the little counter bell, and the

room fell silent. She was standing behind the cash register, her post. I felt proud of her then; she was somehow at the center of this all, this squat gray woman dressed as always in her housedress, her apron, and an unbuttoned green sweater. My grandmother. "I'm not much for making speeches," she said in her rusty scratch of a voice. "We're here tonight because of crime. Let everyone who has a mind to—speak. Let everyone else listen. Sally?"

Sally, standing beside her, also behind the counter, nodded and said simply, "Ideas?"

Mr. Johansson had been sitting on a stool facing them. He swiveled slowly and stood, using his cane, to face the room. I was directly opposite him, standing in front of the middle booth, and for a moment I wanted to duck, for he looked straight at me. "Friends and neighbors," he began. "I have been thinking long and hard, and I have had an idea." Did I imagine the little smile he sent my way? "What we need is a patrol. A neighborhood patrol. To keep our streets safe. I look here and see you, my friends, my neighbors for many years, my customers. Yes? Why should we not live in peace? Why should it be that to walk the street is to put your life in danger, yes? Am I right? But this is wrong. That's not why we invented sidewalks. Not for crime but for people to traverse in peace."

Traverse in peace? I was impressed, and wondered fleetingly who *did* invent sidewalks.

He continued, "Instead of staying off the streets—

hiding at home, afraid—we need to do the very opposite. Use them. Walk them. But before we can do that, we need to secure them."

A man I recognized as Tracy's dad spoke. "I think we should be careful what we get into here. We have police to patrol."

"Police?" Mrs. Mondelli raised her voice in scorn. She was sitting at the table in the window. "And where are the police is what I want to know. We pay taxes, good money. For what?"

As if on cue the door clanged, and Mac walked in. He was off duty, not wearing his badge. Several people laughed at the timing.

"Ah, Michael," Grandmother said. "We were just getting around to wondering about the boys in blue. I'm glad you could make it. Everyone, this is Officer MacAtee, as most of you know. Washco is his day beat."

"Aye, and it's also my home, don't be forgetting." He winked at Grandmother, whose mouth twitched in the slightest of smiles. "I'm as concerned as any about the crime here on Washco."

"And how concerned is the mayor?" Sally asked. "Does she care enough to assign some more squad cars?"

There was a general murmur of assent to this.

"Frankly, I don't know," Mac said. "I myself have been saying the same now for months downtown. Perhaps we should make an appointment and ask her ourselves."

144

"Sounds good to me," Sally said.

Mr. Johansson was still standing, and had apparently grown impatient with the interruptions. He rapped the floor with his cane, and the heads that had been turned toward Mac and the door turned back to him. "We need people on the street is what I'm saying. More police are fine, *if* we can get them. But we need the rest of us out there, on the streets, using them day and night. And we can't do that alone. It's not safe, yes? No. Not yet. Aha. We need patrols, teams. Yes?"

He looked suddenly very tired and sat down. The room was quiet.

Lucy spoke up. "I think we have some good ideas here." Mr. J. threw her a grateful glance. "Let's think about forming teams to—" She frowned in concentration. "To walk Washco. Is that it?" He nodded at her, and she continued, "To use the streets."

I suddenly remembered Grandmother's idea of romance had been to "walk Washco" every night to meet Oscar as he came home from the mill. How long ago that must have been.

"Let me see if I have this straight," said Mr. Bernstein. "You're saying if we just use the streets they'll become safer?"

"Basically, yes," Mr. J. answered, nodding. "But we can't be foolish. There is serious crime here. The object is to keep people safe, not endanger them. Yes? That's why we need to work in teams. For safety."

"No weapons," Sally said. "I won't be a part of anything with weapons."

"Good decision," Mac said. "Most guns are used on the friends and family of the owner. Nobody means that to happen, but it does. I've seen it too much to doubt it."

"Wait a minute," Hannah said. She was on the stool next to Mr. J. and turned to him. "If someone wants to rob us, or worse"—she paused and looked at me, at Tracy behind me—"or rape us, God forbid, how we gonna stop them just by walking? I don't get it."

"The police have to stop it, that much is true," Mr. J. said. He was nodding slowly. "But we have to help. We're the ones who live here, who work here. This is *our* home. It won't get better without us. There's safety in numbers, yes? Besides, think how good it will be for our health, all that fresh air and exercise."

Laughter followed that remark, and I saw Sally and Grandmother exchange a look. There was a question in the look but also something else. Walking Washco was a new idea, and I could tell that both of them thought there was something to it.

"If, while you're walking with your team," Mr. J. continued, "you see something like a break-in or a mugging, then you make noise. As much noise as possible."

"I have a whistle," one of the twins said, standing in the booth.

"I do too," said the other.

"This is good. The right idea." Mr. J. was smiling modestly, but I could tell he was very proud of his proposal. He glanced at me, and I managed a small smile of my own. So he *had* thought of something after all.

WALKING WASHCO was adopted and began that very night. A team made up of Mr. Sibowski, Mr. Bernstein, Shakespeare, and Mac walked for the first time between ten-thirty and one. Lucy offered the center phone as a central switchboard for organizing teams and what came to be known as "the escort service." This was for people like Jessica, who got off work late. The team would meet them and walk them to their cars.

A group was also organized to meet with the mayor. "The more the merrier," Mac urged. "Numbers always have their place in an election year." Grandmother laughed out loud at that.

Even Shakespeare got into the act that night. He offered to speak to Mr. Su about self-defense classes for the teams. The t'ai chi class Shakespeare had been trying to recruit Grandmother for had never gotten enough enrollment. Now he wondered if it might be worth another try. He looked kind of shy to me, standing up before so many people. No, it didn't involve weapons, he assured Sally, and it was, he said with a glance at Grandmother, "an excellent form of lifetime exercise." Mr. J. said he'd give it a try; so did Mr. Bernstein. And when Lucy said she might be interested, he looked particularly pleased.

By the time we locked the door and turned out the lights, it seemed to me a great deal had been accomplished. Several teams were formed that night. Tracy and I were assigned an afternoon shift three days a week. We both wanted nighttime, as it seemed that was when both need and action were greatest, but the grown-ups were against it and wouldn't budge. "Besides," Sally pointed out, "not many people can walk during the day. You're doing us a favor." I doubted it, but there was nothing we could do about it.

Mr. J. called his team the Old Gold Club. It consisted of himself, Hannah, Grandmother, and either Mr. or Mrs. Mondelli. They would walk—"slowly," Grandmother had joked—from eight to nine at night. "If you're at your class," she said, nodding at me, "I'll get Bill to close up."

Bill. All night I'd missed him. Bill, where are you? I asked him again silently. I knew where Jessica was—home in bed. But Bill? His absence was an ache inside me, a hollow place that nothing, no one else, could fill. Bill.

The Sibowskis were the last to leave that night. "If there's really safety in numbers," Sally joked as she strapped Sam into the baby carriage, "we've got it made." Then she turned and hugged my grandmother. "I love you, Maddie," she said in a thick voice.

Grandmother looked surprised and pleased. "Why, I love you too, dear," she answered.

When everyone had finally left, she and I closed up. The shop looked very empty because of how full it had been. "These dogs need a soak," Grandmother said, referring to her feet. She looked sad to me, forlorn in some way I didn't understand.

"Is anything wrong?" I asked.

"I miss Oscar," she answered simply. "He should have been here." Then she shook her head hard, once, and started wearily up the steps.

Bill did not come home that night.

# *fifteen*

I DIDN'T SEE BILL that whole next day until evening. He must have come home while I was out, because I didn't even know he was there until Grandmother sent me up to get him for dinner.

I knocked on his door, but there was no answer. "Bill?" I called, and knocked again. "Bill?"

He made some noise like maybe he was just waking up. "Yeah?"

"Grandmother says to come eat."

Nothing.

"Bill?" I pushed on the door, and it swung open. He lay on his bed with his arms flung over his face. "Can I come in?"

He turned his head just slightly in my direction. "No."

I stood there. "Cab?" he said at last.

"Yes?"

"Go away."

So I did.

Downstairs the restaurant was all excitement. There was a lot to be done, organizing teams, times, routes, escorts. Lucy and Sally, or so it appeared to me, did most of the phone calling and scheduling. Tracy and I did the legwork, and Grandmother sat in the middle and hummed. It was as though Washco had become a big wheel—starting at the river, where the mill used to be and part of it still is, up seven blocks to where Washco Avenue turns—and out from that center point about five blocks in any direction.

Washco. The map of it is firmly imprinted in the soles of my feet, the muscles of my legs. I could walk Washco in my sleep.

WALK WASHCO TO HELP STOP CRIME read the fliers that Tracy and I delivered—this in my so-called spare time. ESCORT SERVICE AVAILABLE, and the phone number at the center. WALKERS NEEDED.

Well, the escort service went over big, I can tell you. At first the daytime shift consisted primarily of Tracy and me. Old Mrs. Somebody needed to go to the bank, we would go to her house and walk with her. A lot of the women who rode the bus and got off at EATS wanted escorts for the rest of the way home. We weren't the only ones walking, though, not by a long shot. Shakespeare walked; so did Lucy and several men from the center. So did Sally and Mr. Sibowski, and Father Paul from Saint Catherine's. So did lots of others. That's what made it work, so many people.

That was the key behind Mr. J.'s idea—numbers. There was safety in numbers, we hoped. And power. Mac, Sally, and a group of others made an appointment to see the mayor of Pittsburgh. She was very polite, "would form a committee to look into it further," came the report.

"Something in me just hates a committee," I heard Mrs. Mondelli say to Grandmother.

"Ain't it the truth," she agreed.

WE WALKED. That very first weekend, the midnight team actually scared off two burglars in the act of breaking into somebody's house. They did it more by accident than design that time. They were walking the street—Bill, Mr. Sibowski, and Shakespeare—when they spotted the two guys around the back of a house. Mr. Sibowski called hello to them, thinking at first they were the people who lived there. When the two didn't answer, they realized something was up and loitered on the sidewalk watching. Then they blew the whistle. Literally. And the burglars fled. Later the police found footprints and some other evidence of an attempted break-in, but nothing was taken. The crime had actually been averted.

According to Mr. J.'s theory, which he explained to me once we were friends again, lots of other crimes, potential crimes, were averted as well just by our presence on the streets. It's hard to know statistically whether he was right, whether we really made much difference. I know it began to feel different. And the mood around EATS became much more positive. There was less head shaking and *tchk*ing of old tongues in the restaurant. For one thing, people were busy. The walks took time, both to organize and execute.

"It's just so crazy it might work" is how Sally put it once, admiringly. "Walk the streets."

Of course, there were lots of gaps in the system. The late-night shifts, which were in some ways the most crucial, were also the hardest to fill. Not a lot of people wanted to walk from midnight to three. Bill did, though. And with a vengeance. He had passed on t'ai chi when he heard about it, but began taking a karate class at Pitt. One night I listened at his door and heard him in there, grunting and kicking. Practicing.

He remained a frightening stranger, often gone, and when there, abrupt and hard. The man who raped Jessica had not been caught; he was out there somewhere, and I think Bill was looking for him. I don't really know what Bill was doing, because I saw him so little during that time. I do know I missed him terribly. I felt a true orphan without him. Despite Grandmother, despite Tracy, despite all of Washco that now felt so familiar, none of it could make up for not having Bill. I grieved for him, and for Jessica, as I know he did, but I grieved also for myself and sometimes cried at night, silently, into my pillow.

*153*

One night, and one night only, after much begging on our part, Tracy and I were allowed to walk the late shift. It was a Saturday. I could sleep in, and she would miss church the next day. We walked with Bill and Mr. Sibowski. The time before midnight we spent in Tracy's room, supposedly resting but actually lying in her big double bed, talking and telling secrets. There was nothing I couldn't say to her, nothing at all, and that kind of friendship was a huge relief.

We set out from the Sibowskis'. The men walked fast; Tracy and I had to hustle to keep up. What a strange sight Washco looked, bathed in the eerie half-light of a faint moon! The buildings I knew so well by day were black shadows, silent and threatening. Mostly we didn't talk, or rather Tracy and I didn't. I could hear Bill and Mr. Sibowski murmuring in front of us, but couldn't make out the words. I tried. I hadn't heard Bill talk much in weeks and wondered badly what he might be saying. But besides their low voices there was only the sound of our shoes on the pavement, of our breathing as we walked.

The first time we made it to the bottom of the hill, the bars were still crowded. By two o'clock, when we'd circled back around after walking many side streets and alleys, the street seemed empty, frighteningly so. The sound of a tin can rolling in the wind made my skin prickle. The remains of the mill stood like a rusting dinosaur, huge in the moonlight, and behind it flowed the river, wide and black and fast.

And then, on a corner not far from EATS, we saw a group of people standing in an alleyway just ahead of us. One of them, a man, had his face painted stark white. As we approached, they quit talking, and the silence became ominous. I gripped my whistle tightly. Bill and Mr. Sibowski slowed until we simply stood there, the four of us on one corner, the clump of them on the other. The silence stretched.

"Oh, hi, Joanne," Tracy said, suddenly. "I didn't see you at first. It's me, Tracy. You know. From ballet class?" She was wagging her eyebrows at one of the girls in the group. As I looked, I saw there were two girls among the crowd of boys. The one Tracy was talking to shifted her feet. She wore black lipstick and a tight black miniskirt with boots, and her hair, also black, stuck out at six distinctly different angles. I would never have guessed she was our age.

The boy beside her said, "Ballet, huh?" and she muttered something to him I couldn't hear.

I became aware of Bill in front of me. He'd been staring carefully at each of their faces, checking them out, I suddenly realized, against the rapist's description he had from Jessica—and storing them away, I knew, just from knowing Bill. He rarely forgot a face, had an excellent memory for them. But no one except Jessica had seen the rapist up close, so none but she could remember him. I understood then, with a jolt, part of Bill's hell. For every face he saw, remembered, pulled out, and went over in his mind, he asked the question *Are you the rapist?* I saw him finish studying them and relax a little. It was just a breath, but some bit of tension drained away from his neck, his shoulders, from the air around him. None of these guys matched, I could tell.

And then we kept walking. "Bye, Joanne," Tracy called as we passed.

"Bye, Trace," a voice called back, and turning to her in the shadows, I saw a slow smile illuminate Tracy's face.

We took a break in the fire station halfway through our shift. I truly loved sitting in their small kitchen drinking soft drinks and eating cake in the dead middle of the night. Some of the firemen joined us, joking with Tracy, who they knew well, and with me, who they were beginning to recognize from "around."

The scariest thing that happened that night happened late in the shift. We were heading up a hill, headed I hoped by then for home, when the sound of a gunshot tore the air. It seemed to be four or five blocks off, and to my vast relief, the wail of sirens started almost immediately. Bill and Tracy wanted to walk over, but Tracy's dad said no; there was nothing we could do.

At three o'clock in the morning, Tracy's dad put his arm around her shoulders and asked, "Sleepy?"

"Not a bit, Dad," she said. "I'm having fun."

"Fun, are you? Well, somehow . . . I hadn't quite thought of it like that." I could hear the humor in his voice. "What about you, Cab? Having fun?"

I considered the blister that was beginning to form on my heel. (My feet were growing again, and my shoes were too small.) I thought of my exhaustion, for it had become hard to ignore. But I answered, "Oh, yes, sir, I'm having a ball," and he laughed.

Bill turned then at the sound of my voice, as if he'd just noticed I was there. He didn't smile, but he didn't scowl either. I considered it progress.

And in truth, I *was* having a ball. Dangerous deepest, darkest night, there's something in me that loves it. I can feel the night in my blood; some excitement rises—to be out in the heart of the night!

I checked on the moon that night, a slivered crown shining luminously white behind the high-flying clouds. If I were a dog, I'd have howled.

# sixteen

MOST OF THE WALKING was not that exhilarating, and night walking, as thrilling as it had been, was also scary and late. That Sunday, I couldn't sleep in. Grandmother, it turned out, had plans for me.

She and I took the bus downtown, and then a trolley over to the Dusquene Incline. We went up the side of the mountain in a little car and we could see for miles, the city and the rivers. Actually, I was amazed to see Grandmother out and about like that. For the whole time we'd been in Washco, she hadn't budged from EATS farther than the front sidewalk, where she stood every day about three with Mrs. Mondelli. She not only had a "going-out coat," she wore gloves!

"You should see some of the city while you're here, Cab," she said as we stood on an overlook on top of Mount Washington.

"I'm seeing it right now," I said truthfully.

"No, I mean go do things. They have a, whatchamacallit, a zoo, and famous dinosaurs."

"At the zoo?" I was kidding, but she missed it.

"No, dear, the Carnegie Institute. You really should see that. It's in Oakland. See over there?" and she pointed. We could see the spires of Pitt, the Cathedral of Learning.

"With you?" I asked.

"No, thank you. I've seen it all and plenty more. But I been thinking I should maybe give you some time off." She eyed me thoughtfully while I tried to look uninterested. "You and Tracy see the sights, huh? Whaddya think of that?"

I thought the idea had definite merit. Time off sounded good to me, although I really didn't mind working at EATS. After I got used to the routine, I wasn't exhausted anymore. Tired, yes, but that only made sleep come easier at night. I was being paid good wages, and tips besides. And the truth is, I enjoyed helping her out. She needed it.

I'd been struck often by the truth of what Mom had said: "Your grandmother needs the help." She was not a frail woman by any means, but she was plagued with arthritis that seemed to be progressing. I could read in her movements the measure of her pain, and some days were worse than others. My being there was a real help to her. I knew it.

As if reading my mind with that uncanny accuracy

of hers, she said, "I been thinking it may be time for me to get someone to help out in the store. Whaddya think? You ain't gonna be here forever."

My ears sharpened at that remark. Did she know something I didn't about my plans, or rather my mother's plans for me? I asked, and she said not, shook her head, and patted my back with her stiff claw hand, gentle as rain. "No, J.L. ain't told me nothing. It just stands to reason." I was glad she thought so.

"No, I just been thinking. I don't appear to be getting much younger, try though I might." She snorted her short laugh in appreciation of her own humor. "Maybe I ought to find someone and break them in while you're still here to help. Whaddya think?"

One of the things I appreciated most about Grandmother was how she was always asking *my* opinion of things. Unlike certain other maternal relatives I could name.

At any rate, that is how I came to have some time off. Which—face facts—between working and walking Washco I dearly wanted. Tracy and I did visit the Carnegie Institute one day, took the bus, two buses actually, into Oakland and saw it all. It does have dinosaur bones, huge ones in an even huger room, and a painting on the wall that Tracy said was magical because no matter how often you looked at it you could always see something new. They have an art museum there too, and a room full of Greek and Roman statues, cathedral fronts. They had a model of the Parthenon, which I read on the little sign is in Athens. Has Mom seen the real one? I wondered. They had case after case of stuffed animals looking very alive, and Indians and mummies, and jewels beyond counting.

The main branch of the Carnegie Library is there too. Tracy wanted a book she couldn't find at the Washco branch, so we went in, asked around, and found ourselves going down and down thin metal staircases to a big basement full of books. She found the one she wanted, a biography of Albert Einstein—her ninth book since class had started. We were in the fifth week. Tracy pursued her reading goal as she pursued Greatness, as she pursued every single day I ever spent with her—with energy, good humor, and high hopes.

She looked the book over doubtfully once we finally found it. "I hope it doesn't try to explain too much," she said.

"Hmm," I said sympathetically. I skimmed through it. "It's got a lot on his childhood, looks like. Maybe it won't be so bad."

We both read the quote on the flyleaf. "Small is the number of them that see with their own eyes and feel with their own hearts. Albert Einstein."

"Maybe it won't be too bad," she agreed.

Later, Tracy wanted to walk over to Pitt. Sally had told her to make sure I saw the International Rooms, each one decorated in the arts and crafts of a different country. I felt nervous there, afraid some-how we would see Bill and he'd be angry with me for being on his territory. "You have a right to be here," Tracy said. "He doesn't own the place, you know." I knew she was right, but was scared of anything that might make Bill more angry, more distant, more strange.

Nonetheless, I wanted to go. I especially wanted to see the Student Union building, where Mom and my father had sat, years ago, and picked Blue Cloud off a map. We did see it too, and sat in a sunny corner in plush chairs as though we belonged. As it turned out, we didn't see Bill at all; we saw Jessica.

Since the rape, I'd seen Jessica only a few times. About a week after it happened, she came into EATS with Bill at about five o'clock, as had been their habit. She looked little to me, shrunken somehow and pale like the waning moon. Except for the still-healing, dark bruise on her face, she looked ghostly white. She sat in the booth twisting her hands on the table, and I saw that her knuckles were swollen and covered in scratches and scabs, a yellow-green swell that made me feel sick to look at long.

As much as I'd thought of her, worried and won-dered about her, I found myself speechless when I actually saw her. To tell you the truth, I was stunned by the magnitude of her pain. It flowed from her in waves. I was horrified that I couldn't think of any-thing to say, but I couldn't. I did say hi, and she did too, but I found it impossible to make small talk with her. She seemed surrounded by an aura of suffering, and it silenced me.

After that first visit, I'd seen her off and on, but not as often as before. She ordered coffee, nothing else, and sat stirring it, listening to Bill or talking in her low voice. They both looked unhappy, strained. She was back in school, I knew, because the little I did know about his life during that time was that they still drove in together in the mornings. And I learned she was back at the Centralia the night Tracy and I went to a movie. We bought our tickets from her. I had a flash of insight as I stepped up to the box office. I suddenly knew how—what's the word? hard? horrible? frightening? dreadful? all of that and probably much more I cannot imagine—but how it was to sit there, night after night, selling tickets and never knowing if maybe the next person who stepped up would be *him*. The rapist remained uncaught, and chances that he ever would be dimmed as time passed, according to Mac.

From the sunken look she acquired, especially around her eyes, I knew she was having a terrible time, a hurting time. You could just see it, plain. Jessica's face once seemed to gather in light and toss it back, sparkling with smiles. Now she neither took light in nor threw it back. She was drawn and dark and moved as though in pain. But she did move. She drew no particular attention to herself; I noticed closely because it mattered so to me. To someone

*163*

who didn't know her, know what she was going through, she looked, I suppose, normal enough. Normal.

Maybe I'm wrong to call any of my brainstorms "a flash of insight," since I don't know for sure, but it was "infeeling" for certain. *Empathy* is a word Gretchen used once in a letter to me about talents. According to her, it is from the Greek word *pathos* for "feeling" and *em* for "with." Feeling with. She thought I could list it among my talents. (This was in reference to what we might "be" when—and if—we grow up.) She has known since she was ten she would be a psychologist, and she's used that as a framework on which to hang whatever life sends her. Tracy has *always* known that she would be great. (What I know is that she already is.) As for me, I would be empathic, so to speak. What good it does to have such a talent is a wide-open question as far as I can tell. Is there a job called empathizer? If there is, the pay is probably crummy.

Anyway, that day at Pitt—I skulking around hoping Bill didn't see me, Tracy showing me the sights, and both of us checking out the college crowd—we saw Jessica walking down a sidewalk about a block away. At first we weren't sure that was who it was, but when she stopped at the light, she turned her head and we knew. She was walking so purposefully we were drawn toward her, and by silent consent neither of us called her name. All right—face facts— we were spying.

We followed her across the wide main street, keeping well behind, and down several blocks into the business district of Oakland. The streets were crowded, and it was fairly easy to keep her in view without being seen. In a way it's dreadfully easy to spy on people. . . .

After a few blocks she turned to the left and continued down a side street. We slowed our pace but turned too and saw her go into a building. We looked at each other, a swift glance that shared guilt and desire both, and walked casually after her.

"You want to go see what it says? On the door?" I asked.

"Do you?" But she knew I did.

"What's it hurt to just look, right?"

"Right."

Nervously we sidestepped closer to the door she'd entered and read the small letters. PITTSBURGH ACTION AGAINST RAPE.

"I guess that means she's getting help," Tracy ventured, and I agreed. We didn't talk much on the bus ride home.

THAT NIGHT, I wrote in my journal, *Dear Mr. Oliver* (despite the fact I thought of him as Shakespeare, in writing I addressed him more formally), *I need a private diary. I can't write in here all the time anymore. Not and let you see it. I have things to say that are—no disrespect intended, sir—none of your business.*

*Fine,* he'd written back. *Write in here when you can.*

I found I looked forward to class despite the fact I almost never participated. Nobody else had read *Jane Eyre* except Shakespeare, and everyone had been duly impressed by its heft and breadth the night I brought it in. I enjoyed listening to my classmates' writing. Mr. Bernstein read poetry almost every class. I loved to hear his choppy accent saying his words, which were most often love poems to his "dear Anna."

Tracy always wrote the longest and, in my opinion, the best papers. It's not just because I'm her friend that I say that; I wouldn't be surprised if everyone agreed with me.

I wrote the assignments Shakespeare gave and continued to write to him in my journal, although I did also buy another book, one with a lock, to keep as a private diary. I knew about snoops. Writing in my journal felt stupid mostly, and embarrassing, but I continued to do it, noticing my life as best I could.

Once, I wrote in my journal to Shakespeare, *I don't see how you can stand having a name like Cranston Oliver. I know this is "pure rudeness," as my mother would say, but you* did *tell us to write in here true thoughts and feelings. Well, that's one of them. If I had a name like yours, I couldn't stand it.*

He wrote me back, *Cab, you'd be amazed what a person can stand. Keep writing.* And I did.

I kept reading too, and after a while I understood

166

enough of *Jane Eyre* that the parts I didn't understand didn't matter very much. The story was getting good.

Virginia was learning to read more quickly than I'd expected. The truth is I figured that if she'd gotten to the age of, what, eighteen? nineteen? and hadn't learned to read, there was probably something wrong with her—that she might learn, but she'd be slow about it. I never considered that it might be because nobody ever taught her. Now, Lucy was reading to her every day (Nancy Drew was their favorite), and Shakespeare was working with her and Mr. Tson privately two hours a week before class. Virginia was beginning to be able to read Mother Goose to Marvel. "Her favorite is 'Doctor Foster,' but I can't make the rhyme come out right," she said, and read it to us in her halting, shy twang.

Whatever it was—Nancy Drew, some magic of Shakespeare's, or, most probably, Virginia's perseverance—she did learn to read. Not well, not at first, but she went from somebody who looked at letters and hadn't a clue to the words they spelled to someone who knew the code. I couldn't remember learning how to read, but it seemed to me doing it in a month was pretty good. And I—face facts—had thought she was slow.

When Grandmother heard that Virginia was reading, she baked her a cake and we threw a little party to celebrate. Lucy and Shakespeare came; Tracy, Virginia, and Marvel; and of course Grandmother and me. Poor Virginia, trying not to smile and smiling big as day for hours on end that afternoon. Marvel sat on the bench beside her, and when Grandmother brought out the cake (we'd put a candle in it to make it festive), Marvel clapped her little fat hands and said, "Yaaaay, Mommmeee."

We all stared. Virginia, for once, was too surprised to cover her mouth.

"Her first word, and it's a sentence!" Lucy said excitedly. "Oh! This is wonderful!" She looked around at us, and I saw her eyes rest on Shakespeare, of all people, who smiled back.

Was I dreaming, or did I not see a distinct, dull blush rise from the collar of his shirt and creep slowly up his neck? I know I did, and I thought of the "signs" Grandmother and I had taken to discussing fairly often late at night while her feet soaked.

Grandmother knew the secret meanings of nose and ear size. She could read character from the set of a chin, the spacing of eyes. She knew how to tell whether a pregnant woman was going to have a boy or a girl, and could spot liver disease and arthritis from thirty paces. She taught me what to look for. She knew weather signs, when to bake soda bread and when not to, and she could predict rain from the color of the river. She, as much as Shakespeare, had taught me how to notice. I did see him blush.

Grandmother set the cake down right in front of Virginia. "We're all proud of you, dear. It ain't every day a person learns how to read. 'Yay, Mommmeee,' indeed," she added, smiling at Marvel.

"Thank you," Virginia said in her small, shy voice. She blew out the candle and cut the cake.

Grandmother, Shakespeare, and Lucy talked with Virginia about her plans. She wanted to get her high school diploma, and maybe go on to the community college if she could. I heard them discussing the possibility of the job at EATS and deliberately went away to avoid hearing more. It made *me* feel homeless to think about the autumn.

Tracy followed me out to the kitchen, where I'd gone to get away. She put her arm around my waist, but we didn't say anything, just stood there together looking out the back window. Bill came in while we were standing there, and although he didn't go out of his way to be friendly, he did say hi as he passed through on his way up the back stairs.

I'd had a letter from Mom, one just to me, on thin blue paper. She'd written on both sides and kept it small. *I am anguished for you all,* she'd written in reference to Jessica. *And you, Cab, in particular, I just miss like crazy. There's so much here I want you to see. In Rome, we threw coins into a fountain and made wishes. My wish was for you, as are many of my thoughts throughout the day.* Typical of my mother, she didn't say *what* her wish was.

*The walks sound like a pretty good idea. Use the streets. Who'd've thunk it? Nonetheless, I want you with a grown-up, preferably a big and strong one. I mean it, Cab. Do you hear me?* It was funny, but I *could* hear her, and could almost see her too, shaking a finger at me to bring home her point—but not really; I still knew I had forgotten my mother's face. *I worry about you out there, as there's no telling what someone might do if they're desperate. And addicts are desperate people. So please, please, PLEASE be careful.*

*I know you worry about Bill,* she'd written. How she knew is beyond me, as I'd written her hardly at all, and then only the most superficial gush I could think of. I wrote it sarcastically, but whether she ever took the insult or not I don't know as she never mentioned it. Her letter said, *But somehow, as sad as I feel for both of them, I know him too well to worry much.* Another enigmatic reassurance from the Queen of Mystery.

She wrote some more about how kind their hosts had been, how lovely to have Jacob so honored everywhere they went. He sent, in her words, and doubtless it was a quote, his "regards," whatever they may be. She sent me lots of hugs and kisses but not a word about plans. Not a word. I wrote a few choice words of my own about her in my private diary. If she ever snoops, she'll get an eyeful.

Tracy suffered from not knowing my fate almost as much as I did, and in some ways that made the whole thing much easier. Once up in her room we'd been listening to the radio and just hanging out when a sad song came on. One about saying good-bye. She started crying. "I don't want you to go," she stammered, rubbing her eyes, her eyebrows drawn in a low frown. She turned away and looked fiercely out her third-story window. You could see, as I knew, all the way down to the river.

I began to wonder about Gretchen back in Blue Cloud. I wondered too if I wanted to go back there. I was very much at home by then in Washco and dreaded being pulled up again. On the other hand I was afraid Mom was going to leave me there, and take up her life with Jacob without me. Tracy shared that fear and sharing it made it bearable.

She and I had other days off and enjoyed every one of them. Grandmother turned serious about my education as a tourist and kept suggesting places for Tracy to take me. We went downtown once, saw the Block House on the point of the rivers, where some general defended his men during some war or other. We walked in and out of skyscrapers and took elevators when we could to the highest floor and looked out.

We also hopped a train. Neither of us had planned it; it was strictly a case of spontaneous action, an opportunity too good to pass up. We were down the hill past where the remains of the mill still stand. There were railroad tracks, and we were following them, not to any purpose that day, just idly walking along. We sat down to rest on a little knoll, and as we sat there a train lumbered by. I mean *lumbered*;

*171*

it was going really slow. And then it even stopped for a while. We were just sitting there talking and resting. But right in front of us stood some boxcars, one of them open and empty. Tracy's eyebrows raised high in speculation. I raised my own, and we got up, came off the hill, and looked a little closer. It really was empty, and the train was really stopped. Why not? We climbed in, both of us grinning like crazy.

And then it took off. With a huge screaming lurch that sent us both flying, the train started up. It not only started up, it gained speed—fast. Before long we were flying, the whistle blowing, the wind zipping by, and the engine roaring. We went a long way before it finally slowed down again. Tracy and I were both getting a little nervous, as running away hadn't been a plan just then and it appeared that was exactly what we were doing, like it or not. The ride had been wonderful, but we decided we better jump off and walk back. Neither one of us would have an easy time explaining our lateness as it was.

Jumping off a moving train is not as easy as it looks in the movies. Even though it was moving fairly slowly when we jumped, it *was* moving. And a boxcar, jumping out, is a hell of a lot higher than a boxcar climbing in. I know. Tracy jumped first and I followed, scared to death but scared worse of being separated from her. I hit the gravelly part of the track and rolled as I thought you were supposed to.

Still, I hurt my knee and my elbow, and we both got scratched up pretty bad.

The walk home that day was long and painful, the evening shift pure torture to work. I hid my soreness rather than try to explain it. I had a feeling Grandmother would not look kindly at my hopping trains on my time off. I lay a long time in a hot bath that night, soaking my sore muscles, and all the time I was grinning. Sweet freedom! If only for a short while, the feel of flying in that open boxcar, farther and farther from home, was one worth having. Even now, the memory of that wild ride makes me smile. It seems the thrill of a thing stays on.

# seventeen

THE CRIME LEVEL on Washco actually did drop some, but it in no way disappeared. One night Mr. Tson came to class limping. He had been attacked near his house the day before. He read a haiku that night, the first thing he'd shared all summer.

> "Down comes whooping crane
> Swooping into the rice field.
> Look! Now he is gone."

I remember it well because I lay awake that night repeating it to myself. It was simple but it haunted me, as did the set of Mr. Tson's hunched shoulders as he limped away from class. Sometime right before I fell asleep, I knew his poem was the shadow of an attack.

Sally came into EATS one morning alone. It was unusual to see her without the twins or at least Sam along, and Grandmother remarked on it. Sally laughed and said, "Didn't recognize me without my appendages, did you? I just needed some time away." I had a fleeting fear that she would go to Europe to "get away" and had to shake myself back to the present.

She was discouraged, she told us, by the mayor's foot-dragging. "Now the committee wants to conduct a study of crime in Allegheny County."

"A study?" Grandmother said, and shook her head disgustedly. "So what's to study?"

This was the main topic of discussion at the next meeting. There were, by then, about forty people walking Washco in groups of three and four. Most groups walked between three and five times a week. Some more, some less. We'd met weekly all month, in different places. That night we were in the library.

"I don't think we're being taken seriously," Sally said. "You don't need to study it real long or hard to figure out Washco's a dangerous place to live."

"Maybe we should invite the mayor to come stay a few days," Hannah said. "Bring the whole committee. They might be surprised how quick they study then."

"No kidnapping," Mr. J. said in his low voice. "But we need something, yes? Something." I could see him thinking. Literally. The lines on his forehead stood out, and it was like seeing the gears in his brain begin to turn.

I looked around the circle. Tracy was sitting close

to me, holding one of Bella's kittens on her lap. Lucy and Shakespeare had come in together, I noticed. So had Hannah and Mr. J., but then, they always did. Grandmother was not there. I could represent us, she'd said, which made me feel good. I'm not too swift with numbers, but I'd say there were fifteen or twenty people present that night.

We were upstairs in the main library, our chairs pulled into a large circle surrounded by books. Sam and Marvel, the twins, and several other children were in the children's section on the other side of the room, being watched by Virginia and supposedly Tracy. But Tracy, like me, wanted to hear what the grown-ups had to say.

"What's discouraging," Mac said at last, "is that actually, if the walks succeed at bringing down the rate of assault and robbery . . . if they work, it's going to work against us in the numbers. You see what I mean?"

"That's ridiculous!" Lucy said hotly. "Why, that would be punishing people for helping themselves." She drummed her fingers on the table and she too wrinkled her forehead in thought.

"It's not the numbers that work against us," Sally said quickly. "It's those fatheads downtown, excuse my language." She looked ruffled and sent a guilty glance toward Father Paul.

There was more silence, and chairs shifted, feet shuffled, someone coughed. From across the room came Virginia's thin voice, singing softly with the twins joining in. "May the circle be unbroken,/by and by, Lord, by and by./ There's a better day awaiting,/in the sky, Lord, in the sky."

"A vigil," Lucy said suddenly.

Sally sat up abruptly. "It's got possibilities." She began to chew on the end of her pen.

"Yeah, you know, candlelight. Singing." Lucy inclined her head toward the soft voices.

"We can stay there until the mayor comes!" Mr. J. added. "Stay for days if we have to."

"I'll make the coffee," I volunteered without planning to, and then blushed when everyone laughed. What was so funny I'm still not sure, but smiles began to zip around the circle and lots of people started talking at once.

A plan was formed, re-formed, de-formed, and finally declared free-form by Shakespeare, who was taking notes that night and trying to keep track of it all. A date was set for ten days away—a Friday night. "If we have to, we stay there all night, all weekend," Lucy said, excitement burning in her eyes.

The idea was to walk, as many people as possible, all at once, down to the mill site and then to stay there, for days if necessary, to publicize the problem. The mayor would *have* to pay attention to crime on Washco and the need for more police if we got enough people out. Or so went the theory. The question was, How many was enough? And could we get them?

Hannah and Mr. J. walked me home that night, the two of them talking rapidly, happily, about the new plans. Mr. J. had signed up for the t'ai chi class, and he demonstrated his new agility to us by whirling around a lamppost. "You see, Hannerl," he said, "you take the class too, and we'll waltz Washco, yes?" She laughed and called him a crazy old man. I walked behind them, scanning the sidewalk for nothing.

I explained what had happened at the meeting as best I could to Grandmother, including the part about us providing the coffee. She said merely, "Huh," and looked thoughtful. I considered sitting with her for a while. She was soaking her feet, it was our usual time for a visit, but I decided instead to go to bed.

Something about the night had depressed me, and I didn't feel much like talking. I sat at the desk in my window and looked out on the street. From there I could see a team of walkers head up toward the hill, but couldn't identify any of them. Craning my neck, I could see the moon, but dimly. It was mostly hidden behind dark gray clouds.

In ten days we would hold the vigil. In two weeks, my mother and Jacob were due back from their trip. In three weeks—and there I stopped. I had no idea where I'd be three weeks from then. The worry of it, and the injustice, burned like bile. Okay—face facts—I felt sorry for myself. "Life is change," Mom had said. Anything could happen. But what would?

As the days wore on, and people around me began to get more and more excited about the vigil, I found myself feeling increasingly out of it. More fliers were made, which Tracy and I, as well as many others, distributed. Sally and Lucy wanted to try and draw people in from the whole city. Crime on Washco was a local problem, but the need for safer streets was citywide.

I got a letter from Gretchen, who had fallen in love with a boy we both used to hate. I really couldn't understand it. She was actually looking *forward* to school starting, if you can believe that.

Sunday morning, five days before the vigil, I woke up late and lay for a while listening to the sounds around me. Although EATS was closed that day, we hardly ever closed completely. I could hear sounds from the restaurant but could not make out what they were. Grandmother knocked on my door.

"Do you have a dress?" she asked, poking her head around.

"Yeah, I have one. Why?" I asked sleepily.

"Bill's taking us out to Sunday dinner. His treat. A busman's holiday for me and you. Okay?"

"Okay," I mumbled, and pulled the sheet over me to consider this development.

Bill was taking us to dinner. In a way it was very like Bill; he used to do that back in Blue Cloud, take Mom and me out and pay for it himself. But he had been so *un*like himself for most of the summer that

*179*

I felt no relief, only a dull knot of anxiety fold itself into its familiar place in my chest.

I remember the time he took us all the way into San Antonio. We'd even taken the little boat ride on the river before we ate at one of the waterfront cafés. He'd been excited then in a secret way, full of smiles and puzzles. It wasn't until we were eating dessert— baked Alaska, which he ordered himself and insisted we eat—that he tipped back in his chair and, grinning broadly, announced he'd won the scholarship to Wisconsin. Mom ordered more wine and toasted him. Even I was allowed a bit. It had been a night of celebration, high good humor, and fun.

But what now? The day would tell. I spent most of it in bed, reading. I'm a slow reader, but I was getting close to the end of *Jane Eyre*. I fell back to sleep sometime in the afternoon and woke up again to Grandmother's knock. "You got an hour," she said through the door. I showered and put on one of my (two) dresses. I was pulling tangles out of my hair, and thinking about cutting it, when I heard the sound of Jessica's voice. It came from Grandmother's room.

Quietly, I listened. Or tried to, but as thin as those walls were, they were just thick enough to make it hard to hear much unless someone talked loud. And this wasn't loud. I heard more the tone—tired, hesitant, low—than the actual conversation. Frustrated, I went into the hall, purposely leaving my shoes off to make less noise.

To my surprise, Grandmother's door was open a crack, enough so I could see Jessica's back bent like a little crescent moon and some bit of Grandmother beyond. I pulled behind the chest of drawers that cluttered the upstairs hallway and crouched. "I can't," I heard Jessica say. "I've tried and I can't."

Grandmother muttered some response that I couldn't make out. Then Jessica started to cry. I saw her back begin to shake. She was wearing a pale lemon blouse. And then I heard the sound of it as the sobs began to come up from deep inside her and out. If you've ever heard anyone cry like that, you know what I'm talking about. If you haven't, I'm not sure I can explain it. It wasn't pretty; they don't cry like that in the movies. Rather it was like a scream mixed with moaning, hoarse and harsh and ugly. Over and over again. Animal sounds, but human. She made no words as she cried, but sobbed for breath and cried some more.

From my hiding place I saw Grandmother pat her lap, and Jessica went to her and curled like a baby against her breast. Grandmother patted her back. "There, there," she said, in time to her pats. "There, there. There, there."

I knew I was seeing something I had no right to. It was much like the day Tracy and I followed her, only worse. But I couldn't help it. I had grown roots where I crouched. In spite of my guilt I needed to know. But there wasn't that much to know. It's not like I discovered some big secret. I still don't know what it was she had tried but couldn't do. I heard only her sobbing, and Grandmother's words. "There, there. There, there."

Jessica began to catch her breath. I could hear her kind of hiccuping as her crying slowed. Then I heard her laugh. Laugh! Grandmother too. "I got your dress all wet," Jessica said, and Grandmother chuckled softly, "Makes no matter." Jessica said something that may have been, "Am I too heavy?" because Grandmother said, "No, pet. Not a bit. Why, you ain't nothing but skin and bones. A strong wind would take you off."

Jessica sighed then, a long quivering draw of breath. Peeking, I could see the sharp curve of her backbone where she lay cuddled in Grandmother's lap. Then, slowly, she got up, and I ducked back, afraid of being seen. I could tell from where she was standing she was looking at herself in Grandmother's big mirror. She stretched her thin neck to its full length and straightened her shoulders, which then sagged, and she sat heavily on the bed. "I wish I could disappear," I heard her say. It wasn't desperate-like, just a plain old fact.

Grandmother didn't say anything for a while, then, "I know the feeling." She too sounded plain, but sad. "But don't." I could hear her usual gruffness, could imagine her eyes twinkling. "We'd miss you."

Jess sighed again, then said, "I'm going to go wash up."

"And I'll go check on Cab," Grandmother said.

I rose quickly to get back in my room, and fell. My feet had fallen asleep. Oh, the indignities of spying! I scuttled, like a crab, back into my room. My feet were two numb blocks of wood when Grandmother poked her head in.

"You ready?" she asked, eyeing my bare feet.

"Yes, ma'am. Almost," I said hastily, smiling dumbly at her as if everything was fine. I could see the wet spot on the front of her lavender summer suit.

Grandmother looked at me steadily for a moment from the doorway. "You okay?"

"Uhhmm-humm." I nodded.

"Well, hurry up, then." The sharpness in her voice was no more or less than usual, but it pushed me over the edge I'd been trying to back off from.

"I *am* hurrying," I yelled at her, and turned away. I tried to walk and stumbled.

"What's wrong with you?" Grandmother asked sharply.

"My feet fell asleep," I said, sitting on the bed and rubbing first one, then the other.

"Huh." She didn't ask how. Just gave me a long seeing look, then headed downstairs.

"I'll be right down," I called after her.

"Huh," she said again, clomping heavily down the stairs in her rubber-soled "going-out" shoes.

I continued to rub my feet, then gritted my teeth in pain when the pins and needles started. I flexed them and put on my own going-out shoes, which were not as comfortable as the sneakers I wore every day. I hadn't much time to collect myself from the whirlwind of emotions I was feeling, but I took a last doubtful look at my face and hair and started out.

I met Jessica in the hall, just coming from the bathroom. Her eyes were red, and the dark circles under them stood out starkly in her freshly washed face. "Hi, Cab. I didn't know you were still up here," she said. Her voice was low but sounded lighter, almost happy.

I was sure my guilt showed plainly on my face. I looked down, then up, then studied the hall telephone like it might be about to go somewhere. "Hi," I said at last, when I remembered.

"So what's that brother of yours up to tonight?" she asked, smiling at me. "Any clues?"

I shook my head and stared at her. Perhaps she didn't know that I'd been snooping, had heard her sobbing those sobs worse than any. Even as I felt relief, which I did, I also felt worse. It was like stealing. I had taken something that belonged to her, and she didn't even know.

"I heard you crying," I said, the words bursting out. I couldn't meet her eyes, but I wanted her to know. Tears of shame sprang up behind my eyes, stinging.

She made a little face and said only, "Did you?" her voice soft, not angry.

*184*

I nodded, and then Jessica did something that still amazes me. She put her arms out and said, "Well, I could use another hug."

So I hugged her. Hugged her hard with all the love and guilt and pain that had been building in me and pressing to get out. She was so thin! Even her collarbone stood out, and the wings under her shoulders made sharp ridges on her back. But she wasn't weak, for she hugged me hard too, just took me in against her bony self and hugged.

We stood apart then and took a breath, wiped our eyes, and laughed a little. She reached over and rearranged a strand of my hair, touching my cheek lightly with the back of her hand. "We better go," she said, and we both smiled.

# eighteen

BILL TOOK US to a Chinese restaurant and ordered seventeen dishes. Okay, I'm exaggerating, but they brought a *lot* of food, and when I thought we were done, they brought more. We were served by two waiters, neither of whom spoke much English. They wore black suits with white shirtfronts, very stiff. The place was packed and rather loud. I could see Grandmother looking around, enjoying herself.

I kept a close eye on Bill for signs of what was behind all this, but couldn't tell much. He was both like and not like himself. He was quieter than he used to be, but not silent, as he had been recently. He was obviously pleased to be taking us out, but not nearly as playful as the brother who'd raised me. He was nicer to me that day than he had been in weeks, and I soaked it in, but all the time waiting for the other shoe to drop, so to speak.

I remembered Gretchen telling me once that people made announcements in public places so that they could control the reactions they got. At least somewhat. No matter how bad the news, the other person was less likely to make a scene in a public place. She'd read some article about it in a psychology magazine.

Sure enough, it was over the fortune cookies. (Mine said, "You will meet a stranger." I wondered if that meant Mom.) Bill sat back in his chair and looked from one of us to the other. Jessica and Grandmother and I looked back. We'd all been wondering.

"I have an announcement to make," he said unnecessarily, and cleared his throat. We waited, and I saw that this, whatever it was, was hard for him. He swallowed once; I could see his Adam's apple bob. "I've decided not to go to Wisconsin this year," he said, and then hardened his face to repel any objections.

"Your scholarship—" I started, but he flicked his eyes at me as though to dismiss the honor he'd worked so hard to win.

"It doesn't matter. I want to stay here," he said abruptly. "That's all. And I'm going to."

With a start, I recognized the family style. Here's what I'm going to do. Not "if you please," not even "What do you think about it?" Just here's what's going on. Deal with it.

"Hunh," Grandmother said, her eyes twinkling. Her mouth twitched in a semblance of a smile, and she reached for her water glass.

"It's because of me, isn't it?" Jessica asked him, looking at her lap. He didn't answer at first, and her words hung there getting heavier by the second.

"Yes," he said at last, and it was practically a bark. "Okay? Yes. So sue me. I want to stay because of *you*." It came out like a terrible accusation, and some heads at the next table turned toward us.

I thought then of what Gretchen had said about announcements in restaurants, and I realized that the person Bill was trying to control was himself, not the rest of us. Himself.

Instead of being frightened by his anger, and he was angry, I found myself getting the giggles. Uncontrollably. I more or less cracked under the strain of the day, the week, the summer, my life. Maybe it was an MSG reaction. Whatever it was, I lost it. At first I had them only a little, just a little case of the giggles, but it got worse as I sat there trying to hold them in. Finally, I snorted into my napkin and turned my head, trying to hide from Bill.

"What is *your* problem, Cab?" he snapped at me.

This struck me as hilarious. "I'm sorry," I apologized, bursting out laughing in his face before I could finish the words. "I'm not laughing at you," but I was, and I knew it, and it still struck me funny. "You're so m-m-mad!" I collapsed in helpless laughter as though this was the funniest thing I'd ever heard. I tried to go on: "But, but . . ." It was no use. I really couldn't stop laughing. "But not at her," I gasped, pointing at Jessica, who was looking at me in alarm. "It's not funny, I know," I said, and then thought that was funny too. "I'm sorry," I squeezed out between giggles. "But you're yelling at her . . . and you're not mad at her. It's funny," I finished, and burst out in a new set of chuckles, muffled in my napkin and trying still to stop.

All three of them stared at me as though I had grown green horns and purple spots on my face. Their expressions made me laugh harder and then slowly, as though in wonder, Bill started laughing too. Then Grandmother absolutely guffawed out loud, spraying water from her glass, and that cracked Jessica up and got me going all over again.

Both waiters came hurrying over to see what was the matter, and that too struck us all as downright hilarious. It was some time before we settled down. I've never had that happen before or since, nor do I look forward to it ever happening again. But there it was. A serious case of the giggles. Thank goodness they're contagious. Bill was smiling when he took Jessica's hand and said, "I'm not mad at you."

"I know you're not," she said, and started giggling. "Oh, don't let me get started again."

"You're not mad?" he asked, looking at me.

"Mad? No," I said, and realized it was true.

"What about you?" he asked Grandmother.

"Well, huh. About you staying? I'm glad," she answered.

"So am I, Bill," Jessica said, squeezing his hand.

"What about me?" I asked, sober at last.

"What about you?" Bill said. "You said you weren't mad."

"I mean, what's going to happen to me, Bill? What about that?" I hadn't meant my voice to sound so desperate.

"Oh, Cabbagehead, you idiot. Mom's not done with you yet. Not by a long shot. Don't you know that?"

I hadn't been so glad to be called a vegetable and an idiot in a long time. I smiled at him, and Bill, my brother Bill, smiled back.

As we were coming out of the restaurant, all four of us saw the moon, which was rounding toward full, shining palely in the early night. Before bed Grandmother pushed something into my hand. It was the strip of paper from her fortune cookie. "A word to the wise is not necessary," it read, and when I looked up, she astonished me by winking.

# nineteen

HAVING BILL BACK made a huge difference for me. My heart was lighter, for he was better. Tracy was glad he was staying on for Jessica's sake. "It makes sense, Cab." I pointed out that he was losing a scholarship, but she shook her head and repeated, "It makes sense." We both knew it did.

As the day of the vigil came near, I too began at last to be infected with excitement. Tracy and I ran errands, hung posters and helped with arrangements, and talked it up with everyone we saw for hours each day.

The plan was for people to gather in the library playground between five and six o'clock. We were hoping to have enough people to slow up traffic on the way down Washco. This was Shakespeare's idea, and I could tell he was fond of it. The group, whatever the number, would gather at the mill site on the river. As this was notorious as a drug drop, people thought it an appropriate place to meet. Saint

Catherine's, across the street, had offered to provide shelter and bathrooms during the night.

The actual day dawned August hot, but dry. That morning in the restaurant no one talked of anything else. "That man is *bad*," Hannah said about Mr. J., echoing the words she'd said weeks before, the day after he was mugged. Now I knew her well enough to understand it as a worried compliment. "He called the national news stations. The nationals. He called New York. Can you believe it?" She laughed, her gold tooth flashing, and shook her head.

"Can your crystal ball tell us what the crowd will be tonight, Hannah?" I asked, mostly joking, although I'd never let her tell my fortune. A part of me was still afraid she could. And I didn't know how to deal with what that might mean.

"Maybe, maybe not. But don't joke about my gifts, young lady. You hear me?"

"I'm sorry," I said quickly, not having meant to offend.

At five o'clock I was still working. Grandmother and I were to close at six and join the march. I saw Lucy and Virginia and Marvel and Shakespeare, and maybe ten other people from the center, round the corner. Sally was there already, with the twins and Sam and Tracy and quite a few more. The playground filled.

Each time I peeked out the window, there were more and more people, and still more coming. And sure enough, I saw news cameras. By six o'clock the people, lined up for blocks, were on the sidewalks waiting. Lots of people had brought signs; a few even made banners. STOP CRIME. TAKE BACK THE NIGHT. SAFE STREETS FOR ALL read a few.

At six o'clock on the nose, as promised, Grandmother turned the key in the lock, and we stepped into the crowd. There were thousands of people! Thousands of them. Tracy was literally jumping up and down in excitement when she found me in the crowd. As we topped the hill and headed down Washco, I realized we were eight or ten abreast for blocks, a slow wave of humanity rolling down that steep street to the river.

Many were old, in wheelchairs or pushing one. Some came on walkers, canes. Many, like Grandmother, hobbled as they walked, but walk they did. There were young people too, and babies, in strollers, in arms, and, like Marvel, who dangled most of the way between Tracy and me, on foot—more or less. It was a huge crowd, which the police estimated at five thousand. I'll say it was a lot of people on Washco.

They came from all over to walk with us that day. It wasn't just Washco that turned up. It was the whole city. Sally and Lucy handed out name tags and markers. Everyone wrote out their name and where they were from. People came from Northside, Southside, Shadyside, Oakland, Squirrel Hill, East Liberty, and more places than I could name in three hours. I'm not kidding. The homeless people were from all over. One man I met came from Nebraska. I'd never met anyone from there before. Virginia, I found out, was from a place called Sassafras, Kentucky. Tracy and I helped her spell it as best we could, but none of us was sure if we got it right.

Grandmother (really the woman is no end of astonishment to me) had on her name tag, "Maddie Doyle, 45th Meridian, North Atlantic Ocean." "Is that where you're from?" I asked her when she taped it on.

"Yes. Born on the boat coming over from the Emerald Isles. A wee thing I was." She spoke in a heavy Irish brogue.

"I didn't know that." Had I ever wondered where she was born? Where she grew up? Had I ever imagined my grandmother as a little girl? Not much. It seemed like a person should know these things about her grandparents.

"Well, now you do," she said, still broguing and with a definite twitch around her sharp mouth.

She could talk in a heavy Irish accent anytime she wanted, but mostly she didn't. Grandmother's speech was a rough accumulation and reflection of her life, most of which, but not all, I now know (45th Meridian!), had been lived on Washco, which itself is a catchall for people from all over.

"Aye," she mused on. "Born in international waters and proud of it." So I wasn't the only one in our family born in transit.

Shakespeare came up to her just then and offered

*194*

her his arm. "Why, thank you," she said, and I heard not brogue but a slight Southern drawl. She had praised Shakespeare to me in private as having "lovely manners." Manners, according to her—and I now saw where my mother had gotten her mania for them—were one of the things that really wore well as you got older. They walked linked like that, arm in arm, a long time, slowly.

The whole walk was slow. These were not marathon runners, nor even among the well-jogged set. This was a walk of the lame, the crippled, the old, the young, and "those who sleep in the dust," as Mr. Bernstein put it. He was there, even on the Sabbath. He didn't often come to meetings if they were on Fridays, as he usually went to temple then, but that night he was there. As were a great many of his friends.

For many blocks we sang songs. At first I felt too shy to join in, but as I heard voice after voice raised around me, and many of them far from perfect, I too found myself singing. "We shall o-ver-come, we shall o-ver-come, we shall o-ver-come some-day . . . . /We shall live in peace, we shall live in peace, we shall live in peace someday."©

Tracy and I sang together and tossed each other small smiles, she with her eyebrows, over Marvel's head. Certain things were harder to say now between us. For girls who so loved words, we found sometimes we couldn't find the right ones. Not to talk about me leaving. The subject began to yawn between us like a chasm we sidestepped and looked away from. It was good to share a song.

The firemen turned out in uniform, black boots shining brightly, blue shirts starched and clean. Hats off when we passed the station. They saluted us. It made me feel humble to see that.

When we reached the mill site, it took a while for people to get spread out and settled. Many had brought blankets for the hard ground, although one section of the area was sandy like a beach.

Lucy had arranged with some of the men at the center for a speaking platform to be built and a microphone set up. Sally and a lot of other people gave speeches; I missed most of what they said because Tracy and I were busy by then, handing out candles. I do know she started it with one of the jokes from the dumb-joke calendar: "I met a man the other day with a dog that can sit at the table with him and play poker. 'What a smart dog!' I said. 'Not really,' he told me. 'When he gets a good hand, he wags his tail.' "

A lot of people laughed, and I heard her say she'd read in the toastmaster's guide to public speaking you were supposed to start off with a joke. "I could die," Tracy murmured, her eyebrows wagging ominously before we got separated in the crowd.

After that I lost track of the speech, although I did hear Sally, and every other speaker, call the mayor, the city council, and all the other politicians to come join us. "Come on over," she said. "Come on over and help us. Please."

That was the idea. To get the mayor to come and make a firm commitment to safer streets in Washco. And if necessary wait until we got it.

We were asking for more police and more street-lights. More jobs would go a long way too, as Mr. J. had pointed out to me many times, but no one held much hope for that. Safety first. That was the issue—safe streets.

I left the speeches to work in the kitchen at the church for an hour. I did keep the coffee coming, and some of it anyway *was* donated by EATS. I packed box lunches that sold for a dollar. You got a piece of chicken, a biscuit, and a potato wedge for your money. Not a bad deal, and we sold a blue million of them that night. The church had bought several bushels of apples that Father Paul and some nuns distributed to the crowd.

Because it was a vigil, there were long periods of time when nobody said anything. As large as the crowd was, it was mostly quiet. Sometimes people were praying, others just sitting, being still, or standing around talking quietly.

As night fell, the temperature dropped quickly, and a heavy mist came off the river, bathing us all in cloudy white. It was from where I stood inside the mist, next to Tracy, that I saw, as in a dream, my mother and Jacob step out of a cab that had drawn up far down the street at the side of the church.

My mother looked around her, her face a painting of pure bewilderment. Jacob paid the driver. The street near the church, with people coming in and out to use the rest rooms or get some food, was busy and quietly festive. A policeman directed traffic. The mist rose in wispy tails, swirling itself around people's legs, the taxi's tires. From where I stood, on the edge of the crowd, the fog was even thicker. People were singing again just then, our voices drifting softly out of the mist. "Kum ba yah, my Lord. Kum ba yah!"

When I saw her, I broke away from Tracy, who was just on her way over to the kitchen to put in her hour of work. "Mom?" I called, and made my way down the crowd until I stood almost across the street from them. "Mom?"

"Cab?" she called back, hearing my voice and straining to see me. Jacob too had turned, and they started across the street.

I will always remember that sight of them, walking to me, hand in hand, peering into the fog. I said it was dreamlike and I mean it, but not in the sense that I was waking from a dream. Rather, it seemed they were coming into a dream to find me.

Mom and I hugged. I found I hadn't really forgotten what she looked like after all, or rather it all came back to me, there in that hug, who she was and that I loved her. No matter what.

"I thought you weren't coming till next week," I said, when I'd caught my breath.

"Well, we weren't, but when we got into New York we heard about this on the news."

"The national news?" I asked, and she nodded. Way to go, Mr. J.! I thought.

"Well, I was getting anxious," Mom said. "I'd heard from Bill about Wisconsin, and then to hear the name Washco on the news, it rattled me. And as it turned out, we could get tickets on the next flight, so we did. And here we are." She paused. "I see you're all right. Are you, Cab?" She held me at the shoulders and looked me over head to toe. "Oh, God, I'm so glad to see you!" She hugged me again.

"I, too, am glad to see you," Jacob said softly, and lifted his hat. "You have gathered a big crowd, ja?"

"Ja," I answered, smiling.

"Where's Mama?" Mom asked, looking around us in the huge crowd.

"She's here somewhere," I assured her.

Tracy came over, and I introduced her. I could feel her stiffness, and she had no time to stay just then. We arranged to meet later at the speaker's platform, and she went off to the kitchen, her gait jerky, head down.

Mom, Jacob, and I walked slowly through the crowd, keeping together. And then, through a break in the mist, I saw Bill and Jessica far ahead of us. He was standing with her tucked under his shoulder.

She huddled into him as though tired, and looked rather frightened, pale. I pointed them out to Mom, who began to wave.

I wondered then what Jessica looked like to someone like Mom, who had never seen her before. Mom had never met the girl who Bill first brought home, the beauty whose light had sparkled around her. She would never know the Jessica who had not been raped.

The five of us continued together and finally came upon Grandmother, who was sitting rather stiffly on a blanket near the front. "Mama!" Mom called as she went to her. "Have you turned into a rabble-rouser in your old age?"

"You got that right, rascal. Come join us," Grandmother said, and patted the blanket beside her. Mom and I sat down while Bill, Jessica, and Jacob hovered above.

News had just come from downtown that the mayor was on her way to Washco. A cheer rose up from the candlelit crowd behind us. "Now we'll see, J.L., if we get any action," Grandmother said. "Oh, how I do wish your father could see this. It would tickle him pink."

"It would, wouldn't it?" Mom smiled.

Grandmother and Mom visited in this way for only a few minutes, but the question that had been growing in me all summer was swelling by the second. "So what's the plan?" I said at last, when there was finally a break in the talk between them.

*200*

"Ah, yes," Mom said, and put an arm around me.

"She has been wondering, ja?" Jacob said from above, and I felt his hand on my head.

They did have a plan for me. We were moving, the three of us, to Brussels. Belgium. I was, it turned out, already enrolled in the American high school there. School was to start in two weeks. Jacob had accepted a position at the conservatory of music, and we would live there at least for the next year. Such was the plan.

"Oh, Cab, I think you're going to love it. Brussels is *so* beautiful. Especially the old part. And the museums, and castles, Cab. Well, you'll just have to see it. I can't wait." Mom talked on and on; I missed a good deal of it, hearing only her voice, not the words as they fell around me.

I lay back on the blanket and shut my eyes. The ground was hard and rocky underneath us, but the image I had was of myself as a child, as I would lie on my bed and Mom would snap the sheet above me. Down it would come, billowing, warmth and softness all around. For a moment I just let that sheet descend on me, felt its sweet breeze, and knew that indeed I hadn't been forgotten.

The next few hours were hectic beyond recall. Tracy got back from the kitchen and found us just as the mayor was arriving. I had time to whisper to her only that I was going to Belgium, or so my mother had said. It was a possibility we'd completely overlooked in our speculations about my fate. "I guess I'll learn French," I told her.

Her face crumpled a moment, and she turned away. She stared into space as though she were blind, but I saw tears roll down her cheeks and reached for her hand. "It's just I'm going to miss you so much," she said at last in a tight voice.

"I know," I answered. "I feel the same."

The mayor's speech was short and sweet. The news cameras whirred, their trucks casting huge lights and leaping shadows on us all. Washco would get more police, and more streetlights too. Not only that, but the mayor was adding Washco to the list of neighborhoods that would be getting the still-experimental horse patrols. Stable areas had already been found in the deserted warehouse just across the street.

Horses! Stables! Tracy's eyebrows danced in delight. She flashed me a grin, even as her tears were still drying, and we joined in the cheering. This unexpected piece of good news came when she needed it. "I'm gonna get a job there, wait and see if I don't. Whaddya think?" She nudged me in the ribs.

"I'm sure you will," I said, and felt a little jealous. I knew more about horses than she did, but maybe, I admitted to myself, remembering the walls of her room, she loved them more.

There was a further announcement by a city councilman that what was left of the mill was being considered as a recycling plant for newspapers, cardboard, and things like that. "We need work!" the chant went up from the crowd. "We need work!" I looked and saw Mr. J. shouting away. He spotted me and waved. I joined in at the top of my lungs.

Father Paul made an announcement that the evening would adjourn with a prayer service across the street in the chapel. It was dedicated to the victims, both living and dead, of violent crimes.

At its conclusion, Jacob, who had been persuaded by Lucy and Shakespeare, played a piece by Bach on the church piano. I was part of the crowd still outside on the street. We listened in silence as he spun out the music. We started back up the hill with those notes, so simple and pure, still in our ears. Over us rose a full moon, and stars, sparkling beautifully in the black night.

I walked with Tracy, up ahead of Mom and Jacob and Grandmother and Bill and Jessica and Sally and the sleepy twins and the wide-awake Sam, ahead of Hannah and Mr. J. and Lucy and Shakespeare, behind Mr. and Mrs. Mondelli, Mrs. Dinsmore and Mr. Tson from class, and hundreds of others. Amid and among them all we walked home. I told Tracy that night what Bill had told me, about the moon. How it was the same moon all over the world and that I would be checking on it, thinking of her, and for her to do the same.

# twenty

MY LAST FEW DAYS on Washco were
spent like coins that, once they start slipping through
your hands, slip faster until they're suddenly, too
soon, gone.

Tracy announced to our class that it was my last
time, but it turned out everyone already knew.
Shakespeare had bought me a book, my own copy
of *Jane Eyre*, and each person signed it. Mr. Bernstein had also written out a long list of cities and
places I had to see now that I was going to Europe.
I promised I would do my best. Mr. Tson smiled
and bowed and wished me well; Mrs. Dinsmore
hugged me. Virginia made me promise to send post-
cards, and Shakespeare, at the very end, shook my
hand and said, "Keep writing, Cab."

Mom and Jacob stayed only a day before flying
back to New York to make arrangements for moving.
I was to meet them there in five days' time and fly
to Europe. Before they'd left, they'd settled some-

thing with Grandmother, the details of which I don't know, but which meant that she could afford not just to hire Virginia, but someone else as well.

"I'm getting old," she said to me my last night there, her feet soaking in the tub. "They think I need the help, and I can't say as they're wrong." She blew out a great sigh. "Still, it's gonna take a while to get used to the idea of a wealthy son-in-law." She paused and twitched her mouth. "Somehow, though, I think I'll manage."

We'd both laughed and talked some more. We stayed up late that night discussing signs. "I'll keep an eye on Bill for you, Cab. And Jess. Not to worry. We'll be in touch," she said. Bill was to go on living there, having transferred to Pitt.

I told her to keep an eye on Lucy and Shakespeare. "I see signs," I told her. I didn't tell her Tracy and I laughed ourselves sick the night before, trying to imagine what Lucy might call him in moments of passion—Cran? Cranston? Oh, Crannie?

Tracy and I said good-bye at last with a silent hug. No words could have saved us anyway by then; the truth was I was leaving and it hurt. Tracy knew who both her parents were, she knew her address, and had had the same phone number all her life. None of that could I lay claim to anymore. But she'd needed me as much as I'd needed her. We were friends, plain and simple, or as simple as anything would ever be again for either of us.

I hope she knows I think of her when I'm checking

on the moon. A part of me will always be on Washco. With her. The summer we were both thirteen.

Before I left, Mrs. Mondelli pinched my cheek. "So there you are." She pointed to me as if I'd been hiding. "Don't make yourself such a stranger."

"I'll try not," I said, knowing in my bones that stranger was exactly what I was about to be all over again. In Brussels this time. Wherever that was.

"You be a good girl," Hannah instructed, enveloping me into her ample chest and squeezing hard.

"Yes, ma'am," I said into her blouse.

Mr. Johansson came by early especially to see me off. He gave me a picture of himself, real shyly like he didn't know if I'd want it. He was standing tall in it and looked younger than he really was, although still white-headed. I thanked him, and we too hugged. I keep that picture of him at my desk and am looking at him now. He helps me think.

At the last minute I found myself alone in the kitchen with Grandmother. "Tell me," I said, "why didn't you see us all those years? Why?"

She turned and looked at me hard, and then nodded as though she'd settled something in her mind. "Huh," she said, "you got a sense of timing after all, don't you, my girl?"

I smiled modestly in case this was a compliment, which I halfway doubted from the look on her face. "But why, Grandmother?" I really wanted to know.

She took a deep breath and said, "Because I was, and to some extent still am, a stupid, stubborn, prideful old woman who got her feelings hurt when your mother wouldn't come home to me after your . . . your father left. And of course until here lately we ain't been a family with much money for getting around." She looked straight at me, pinning me in her narrowed eyes. "And in your case, my dear, I regret it. I wish I'd known you sooner, but there it is. I'm glad enough to know you now. Does that satisfy you, my curious customer?"

I nodded, but in truth felt overwhelmed by this, and a bit ashamed of myself for bringing such a thing up at the last minute. Whatever else she was, she wasn't stupid. "Grandmother, I'm sorry. Don't say anything else."

"Well, I've one more thing I aim to say, and this is it. You have a home here, Cab. Anytime, no questions asked. Got it?"

"Got it," I agreed.

Bill and Jessica drove me to the airport. He teased me about Belgian boys. Said they had the reputation of being the world's greatest lovers. "They do not," I replied finally, but at first I'd believed him and found myself blushing. He helped me check my bags. Our dad's painting of Bill and the wildcat was tucked safely between my clothes. If Duke ever comes looking for me in Blue Cloud, Gretchen will tell him where I am. Plus we left word at the post office. Most likely he won't. But you never know.

And then it was over—the very last good-bye, the last hug, and I was alone, flying into the future with only myself to make sense of it all. I felt very much alone, and very grown-up. I made that trip in sober contemplation of my life.

I have been in Brussels for a year now, or almost as much. It is nearly summer again, May. I've tried to tell this as it was, as I knew it then and see it, hear it, feel it, and remember it now. I've tried to be honest in all cases, and at times it's been, shall we say, difficult?

I've written this story to help me remember it. And to understand. It came to me at last that no one but I could understand my own life.

I flew off that day into a future as blank as the flat blue sky we headed into. As the plane took off, I felt full of fear, but also alive to possibility, and, for what it's worth, completely myself. Flying toward fall, I saw the summer hang, like a berry dripping with juice, unbearably sweet, and then as the wheels of the plane left the ground, full at last, I saw it pull away and fall from the vine. Into my lap, so to speak.

*About the Author*

JENNY DAVIS has published two earlier YA novels, the well-reviewed *Good-
bye and Keep Cold* and *Sex Education*.
She lives with her sons in Lexington,
Kentucky, and teaches English and sex
education at The Lexington School.